Tru felt an arm slide around her waist.

C. B.'s touch welded Tru to the spot where she stood. Tru's body shivered from the combination of the cool, dank basement and the desire to respond in kind to C. B.'s touch.

"You're freezing," C B. said as she felt the shiver run through Tru's body. "Come here," she invited and opened her heavy firefighter's coat.

Before Tru could protest, before she could decide that she should protest, C. B. gently pulled Tru toward her and tucked her inside the coat. Tru rested stiffly against the warmth that had been offered.

"I've had just about enough of this," Tru said with a menacing tone.

"I thought . . ." C. B. said, faltering.

"I've had enough of this to know I want more."

River QUAY

Janet McClellan

THE NAIAD PRESS, INC.
1998

Printed in the United States of America on acid-free paper
First Edition

Editor: Lila Empson
Cover designer: Bonnie Liss (Phoenix Graphics)
Typesetter: Sandi Stancil

Library of Congress Cataloging-in-Publication Data

McClellan, Janet, 1951–
  River Quay / by Janet McClellan. — 1st. ed.
     p.   cm. — (A Tru North mystery : 3)
  ISBN 1-56280-212-7   (alk. paper.)
   I. Title. II. Series : McClellan, Janet, 1951–   Tru North
mystery : 3.
PS3563.C3413R58   1998
813'.54—dc21   98-13233
                                              CIP

Each life inexplicably shown,
time's breath in pitch and twine,
the keen observer regards our mind,
to discover the way winds have blown.

J. E. McClellan (1997)

Acknowledgment

To all the women who make Naiad possible,
thank you.

About the Author

Janet E. McClellan began her career in law enforcement at the age of nineteen. During the next twenty-six years she worked as a narcotics investigator, patrol officer, detective, college professor, prison administrator and, more recently, chief of police in a small Midwestern town. When not writing mysteries, she spends her time traveling and investigating the mysteries of Dallas, Texas; Kansas City, Missouri; Eagles Nest, New Mexico; and other points on the compass, particularly North.

Chapter 1

Tru North ran through the darkened streets of the plaza in Kansas City, Missouri. The streetlights cast high, dim halos above her and scattered their light softly against the early morning fog. The weak beams wavered and strained, never quite managing to meet the pavement beneath her feet.

There was some place she needed to go. She had to get there, and she had to hurry. Her feeling of urgency, coupled with the nagging questions of where and when, fluttered against her skull like a dull ache. It drove her on.

Soft, cooling breezes of October clung to her skin as she ran past the black-eyed storefronts. Steam, formed between the warmer street and cool air, rose to meet her swiftly passing feet. The mists floated around her face and hands, making her skin sparkle with a thin sheen of dew as she hurried toward her destination.

Her legs churned, and in her haste she sensed herself as taller, more elongated than her shorter frame could account for. Her bare feet slapped almost soundlessly against the pavement, carrying her slight weight easily across the cobblestones. Breathlessly, she pushed on into the ending night as the first soft rays of morning crept slyly up into the sky.

Tru glanced at her pounding feet and stared wonderingly at her clothes. She thought she remembered leaving the police department, but the faded blue jeans and pink long-sleeve shirt were unfamiliar. A finicky dresser, she knew she would never wear her knockabout clothes to work. It was not like her, but there they were, and where were her shoes? She tried to remember, but the urgency scratching at the back of her mind let the thought slip away. She had to hurry.

"What am I doing?" she complained and let the question trail a thin stream of vapor from her mouth. The empty sidewalks and vacant-eyed shop windows seemed to whisper her question back to her.

Hurry, a small, rasping voice snaked through her mind as she pitched herself across the park and up the slopes of Westport. Peevishly, her eyes darted down an alley as her feet turned to follow her gaze.

Tru sensed the end of her destination. It was there. In there. Something was waiting, and she ran headlong into the dark. The terrifying darkened form that had been waiting and hiding rose to meet her startled gaze.

Screaming fear and anger, she raised her hands in protest and struck out at the rushing black tide that threatened to consume her. Her feet frantically twisted and turned beneath her as they tried to take her back the way she'd come. She slipped, fell, and scrambled upright, kicking and warding off the suffocating entity.

A dark pealing enveloped her from deep inside the terror. With her heart threatening to pound free from her chest, her arms flailed in protest at the impending doom. Tru lunged away from the terror. Crashing thunder roared as sharp pains stabbed into her wounded head. Mystified, Tru struggled out of the bedsheets and stared wonderingly around her bedroom. The phone on her nightstand rang out again.

"I've been working too hard," she muttered in exasperated gasps as she tried to crawl back into bed and snatch at the perturbing phone.

Chapter 2

The middle floors of the seven-story structure had been partially engulfed in the blaze. Wherever there was a structural weakness, chimneylike opening, or lack of firebreak, the flames licked and worked their way up toward the next floor. The fire had begun to spread out the windows and over the bulky ledges, licking menacingly toward the floors above. Orange and white flames fed themselves on the air and ancient beams as they roared their release into the weak dawn.

Two ladder companies with their complementary

hose trucks had arrived hours earlier and fought valiantly. The building was old, dry, and weakened by years of near vacancy. Only chance and carefully-aimed, jetting streams of water were keeping it from becoming the flaming tinderbox that circumstance had ascribed for it.

On the face of the old, brown-brick building, the name GENESSE EXCHANGE twinkled in bas-relief against the glare of the flames. Wide arching windows and ornate stone struts two feet out and away from the side of the roof adorned the building, and massive granite ledges defined every story. It had been an impressive piece of work in its heyday in 1901. The vacant gaze and darkened streets of the Kansas City West Bottoms building spoke of neglect, decay, and oblivion as fire raged within.

Few people in Kansas City, ever gave a thought to the Bottoms. They'd forgotten that under the bluff where the Kaw and Missouri Rivers met in its smooth-hipped curve had been home to the city's industrial strength. The Bottoms had boomed for 120 years. It had been the backbone and home to the largest stockyard in the United States. That is, until the flood of 1951 and the economic busts began to accompany the shame the city felt for its rough imaged past. The city changed its image finally by pretending the past had never existed.

Kansas City was a little ashamed of its rural past and the once prevalent smell of manure that had been the smell of money. The city was ashamed to be remembered as a cow town and preferred that citizens and tourists alike think of it only as water fountains and glass towers. Businesses had steadily fled. Gone were many Bottoms banks, stock exchanges, trucking companies, and restaurants. A few long-time companies had hung on. A few restaurants specializing in steaks or home-cooked meals, a trucking and storage company or two, seed companies, and a mixture of stray prostitutes. Then in the early nineties some vacant buildings had been partially refilled by enthusiastic investors, renovators, and hungry artists. They came looking for and found cheap rent, and the West Bottoms was a perfect or near-perfect location.

This was not the area of distinguished or flashy architecture. There were handsome brownstone and redbrick buildings, but they impressed more by their sturdiness and integrity than by grander esthetic principles or the use of opulent materials. The buildings were erected for thoughtful, sensible reasons, and as such they outlived most of the fancier structures that once dotted the Bottoms.

For the last twenty years, most people in and around the area thought the West Bottoms was spooky. That was particularly true when October arrived. The old buildings were turned into tensile terrors and hell houses for the teenagers and twenty-something set. Kansas City played to a monthlong celebration of Halloween, which was when most people were right about the spooky feelings. During Halloween, the West Bottoms seemed to call out to the night and its mourned past. One could almost hear the beseeching whispering through the dusty, weed-strewn streets in broad daylight. The nights made the haunting more real and irreverent to the bright contrast of the daytime. Things were said to happen where superstition was reborn and fear breathed mystically down revelers' backs.

In its distant past, the West Bottoms had employed over 25,000 citizens from either side of the Missouri River. Now it was lucky to employ several thousand. Like an old lover, abandoned for the advance of gray and the onset of wrinkles and weight of each successive year, the West Bottoms had succumbed to neglect. It was deserted by improvement monies and all but forsaken for the perfect complexions of newer diversions. The Bottoms languished.

C. B. Belpre sat in the back of the arson investigation van, watched the fire, and wanted a cigarette. She'd been unconsciously fumbling in her jacket pocket before she remembered she did not carry them anymore. She silently swore her irritation at her dutiful response to a physician's warning. Cold turkey after twenty years of habit had been difficult. Her desire to uncomplicate her life and her long internalized habit of will had made the process a little easier. Being the benefiting descendant of a family with old money, she carefully chose her habits, interests, and desires.

She watched the weakening fire cook the sky and the billowing smoke towering over the puny efforts of the firefighters below. Over the last three hours, she had given mute witness to the consuming fury as she felt the tugging in her body to do more than stand by as a spectator.

C. B. knew what the firefighters were facing. She remembered the blinding, choking smoke, the anxiety associated with the physical exertions, and the exhilaration of personal and team efforts to bring the beast under control. It made her fidget in minute spasms of muscle animation along her arms and legs.

Her eyes danced in anticipation and recognition of intensity from one fire-fighting point of attack to another. She was with the ladder companies in spirit and ingrained habit but removed from the vigor of their direct physical involvement. C. B. chafed under the forced absence on the front line. That absence had become her constant regret and longing.

If anyone had been observing her rather than watching or concentrating on the controlled frenzy of the firefighters, they would have seen a woman in deep concentration. They might have noted her statuesque form but have missed the underlying whipcord strength. They would have seen an easy, lounging figure but not recognized the disciplined mind and power coiled inside. If they had stood close enough, they might have noted the salting and peppering of the dark brown hair, the softly set lines at the corners of her brown eyes, and the sculptured planes of her face. Someone might have noted her large hands with their long fingers clasped across her upraised knee that hinted of stamina.

A very careful observer might have sensed some intensities of her personality even as she lazed against the door frame of the van. But they would have to have been attentive, a special kind of observer, and moderately intense themselves.

Even those who had an opportunity to stand very close might not have seen through the veneer she offered to the general bystander. Rather, they might have perceived a battle-weary character, a veteran of time and circumstance. If they were a bit insightful, they might have seen a little something more of themselves.

C. B. reached again for the cigarette that wasn't

there and frowned. When she had been a firefighter, she'd found the aftermath had been a great time to light up. Not knowing what to do with her hand, she reached up and ran her fingers through her hair. It didn't help. Fighting fires was what she wanted to do, what she'd enjoyed, but it was beyond all practicality now. Seven years ago she would have been among the eager Young Turks whom she now watched throw themselves into the fiery furnace. She would have been at one with them, directing their energies with the experience of her years. She would have been sure, strong, and agile. If that fateful fire and a blaze-weakened floor had not betrayed her, she would have been showing the pups how to do it. *If* she had not fallen ... *if* she had not been injured. But she had and she was.

After the fall, after the bone-cracking landing and flesh-searing flames, she had been left to face a long series of surgeries and equally painful recoveries. She had regained her strength and confidence, but the fall had laid claim to her agility.

She shifted in discomfort and watched the orchestrated firefighters' daring and eased her aching left knee from the angle she had propped it in. The tiny, constant ache and thin lines of long-healed scars were the reminders of why she waited impatiently on the sidelines.

The years of recovery and the struggle to regain and remake her fractured self-image had softened and relaxed the sharper angles of her face. Tenderness and understanding showed itself now, where only challenge had been present before. Her body was a little fuller, less rangy and raw. It could yield itself more easily under a lover's touch rather than resist the mutual needs. A dawning acceptance of an internal integrity of her identity had soothed the sharp edges on which she and old lovers had once cut themselves and bled. The passing of long healing seasons and the simple passage of time had left her whole, grounded, and comfortable. Where she had once been considered threatening and overwhelming, she was now more often regarded as compelling or intriguing. It had taken her almost forty-two years to gain a place of peace with herself. The accident and its recovery had hurried the process a little. It was a realization and reality for which she was mostly thankful.

Shifting her attention to the street, C. B. watched as spectators drifted in and out of the scene. The curious and owners of nearby properties slowly drove by, halted, and watched in interest or anxiety as the fire fought the efforts of water and venting.

She stood up, cautiously stretched her leg, testing by habit for potential weakness, and grabbed the telephoto camera from the storage box inside the van. Shutting and locking the van doors, she set the camera on auto-focus and moved slowly toward the tight clusters of sightseers. The whirl and snap of the camera exposing its film and collecting the populated scene was masked by the shouting of firefighters, the din of the trucks, and the gutting roar of the fire. She easily wove in and out of the shadows of the late night, waiting, watching, and zooming the lens in on faces that seemed too transfixed and on the license plates of those who could not be bothered to get out and stand.

C. B. reloaded with color film and aimed the camera at the building. She rapidly snapped shots of flame and smoke as they poured out of the structure. Later she would look at the faces and match license plates to people. The comparisons would tell her if those faces had ever appeared in other fire scenes or if they were locally known arsonists. Later she would talk to the first responding firefighters and witnesses to find out if they recalled the earlier colors or odors of smoke and flame. The fault and cause would be decided to the satisfaction of the state's chief fire marshal, arson unit manager, and any insurance company who held a policy in the old edifice.

It was C. B.'s job to make sure that the truth was discovered, that fault was laid at the right door, and that no one paid unless there was clear, unmitigated proof that arson was not a factor. An arsonist's motive and pathology would be sorted out from any structural design or flaws of the building.

A few hours later, as dawn broke over the city and the sun sneaked across the wide flat plain of the West Bottoms, early morning commuters would have noted that the fire had been beat. The old structure stood mute, dripping rivulets of water and retreating streams of acidic vapors into the morning air. C. B. put on her boots, pulled the black leather backpack across her shoulders, grabbed a large toolbox and giant flashlight, and started across the street to enter the disfigured building.

"C. B.! Over here," a deep male voice called to her.

C. B. turned and saw Fire Chief Daniel Flanders waving to her. He nodded grimly at her as he turned back to the two firefighters who stood with him. As she walked toward the group, C. B. noticed the firefighters glance at her apprehensively and avert their eyes.

What the hell? C. B.'s curiosity quickened her otherwise deliberate gait. "What's up, Flanders?" she said as she approached the weary trio.

"Go ahead," Flanders urged the men. "Tell her what you found."

"A body. Least I think it's a body. Tim saw it first. He thought it was some kind of weird mannequin. Didn't ya, Tim?" Mike O'Bannion said, nudging the man to his right.

"Yeah, yeah . . . I did. It's not like you'd be expecting anything else to look like that," he responded gradually.

"Where?" C. B. asked smoothly.

"Sixth floor, near the northwest corner. Not burned, but the heat got to it all right. Crispy . . . you know . . ." Mike's voice trailed off to a whisper.

"You'll have to write it up for me. What you heard, felt, saw in the area, everything," C. B. directed the men. She ignored Mike's paling face as best she could. She did not want him to feel any worse than he did. She studiously redirected her orders to the men to innocuous bureaucratic requirements. Not every firefighter's career would bring them face-to-face with the disasters of heat and flame on flesh. It was not a good thing to see. The encounter would have been unexpected and loathsome and would raise sympathy for the poor bastard who'd been charred.

"We know," Tim interjected as he grimaced. The image of piles of paperwork, which he didn't want to complete but knew he would, danced in his head. Regulations were regulations, and you never argue with the arson investigator, particularly Investigator Belpre.

"That it?" C. B. asked.

"That's not enough?" Flanders snorted. "Looks like you'll get to share this one with some hotshot in blue."

"Right," C. B. said as she tried to shrug away her annoyance at the thought of having a police officer working alongside her. "But I'm not going to call the police department before I know whether it's a body or a figment of these fellows' imaginations. And if I heard you two correctly, you're not very sure. Are you?"

"Pretty much," Mike agreed.

"I didn't want to get that close to it. Evidence. Didn't want to screw things up for you or the cops," Tim explained.

"So, can I go ahead and go in there now?"

"Be my guest," Flanders said, shaking his head at her. "Damned if I know why you like this sort of thing."

"It's not a matter of *like*, Dan. It's a matter of *have to*. Remember. Neither you nor the city would let me retire on partial disability. So here I am, wandering through the messes you leave behind and the aftermath of torches."

"You wouldn't have known how to handle retirement. Be honest, C. B." Flanders gibed kindly. "Fine-looking woman like you. At forty-five, you're still a pup. That's too soon to withdraw from the world."

"I know exactly what I'd be doing. I'd be fishing

clear mountain waters and living in a cabin with no one to irritate me. But, not me, oh no, I'm slogging around in muck and mire picking up after you and your kids," C. B. declared as she turned away.

"You love it," Flanders called after her.

C. B. ignored Flanders's remark and continued her way back toward the gaping soot-sodden maw of the building. It would take her two or three hours to carefully pick her way through the building in the initial search. Notes of suspicions, unusual placements of items, the sweep and chimney-effect of elevator shafts and stairways would be noted first. Then there was caution. The fire was out, the building secure, but that didn't mean that all the danger was past. Fire weakened everything. And what fire didn't scar, the water and venting techniques of the firefighters did. She moved cautiously. She didn't want to fall through another weakened floor or impale herself on a piece of debris.

She was in for the search of the building. She was looking for any clue, any item or piece of evidence that might indicate that this was not an act of God or faulty building codes. It was a legal search. The fire department was still on the scene, and according to *Michigan v. Clifford* she had not violated the reasonable time period of entry. Holding to the rules established that anything she might find or locate in plain view and exigent circumstances could and would be used as evidence in court to convict a person of arson.

She would stay as long as she needed to. It was her habit, that once she entered a building where cause was unknown, she would not leave until she was satisfied. Satisfaction came when she found the origin and established or eliminated arson. Simple in concept. Long in time. Her investigative techniques meant she took a little longer than did her colleagues in the Arson Investigation Unit, but the accuracy of her results warranted and proved her care. The state fire marshal and the court judges never argued with her results, so they were hard pressed to argue with her techniques.

Three hours later, she found the body on the sixth floor. When she saw it, she understood why they had been reluctant to assert that the figure in the corner had ever been human. It hung from ropes attached to a crossbeam, a leather hood over the face, and the body was partially covered in what appeared a short-sleeve wet suit. It looked as though it would collapse to the floor rather than continue to lean in its masquerade of submission.

C. B. cautiously approached the figure and the area surrounding it. Ten feet from the body she stopped as her nose was hit with the full force of the fetid stench of broiled flesh and saw the faint, bubbled marring on the forearms.

Her lips curled in revulsion. She backed away and resigned herself to the overdue call to the Kansas City police department. It was definitely a time for sharing.

Chapter 3

"You've got to be kidding," Detective Tru North said as she turned the car at the corner of Ninth and Genesse and saw the burned building.

"About what?" Tom Garvan asked without changing his hangdog expression.

"That," Tru said pointing at the building as she pulled the car over to the curb. "I'm not dressed for this. I just got these out of the cleaners," she complained, waving a hand at the dark blue jacket, white blouse, light gray slacks, and matching London Fog coat.

"Getting finicky, are we?" Garvan chided.

"Well," Tru said turning to him. "Maybe a little. Although a protective jumpsuit seems more in order than these. Really, the blouse is silk. If I ruin my clothes, do you think the department will let me charge it off to expenses?" she asked, laughing lightly.

"You can try anything, but that doesn't mean it will work." Garvan shrugged the shoulders of his rumpled jacket. He had four suits that he habitually wore to work — all dark gray, all off the rack, all purchased on the same day ten years ago. They would be replaced only if a serious disaster, like lightning, ever struck him. His suits were plain, basic, and dependable, even if they received irregular intervention by some dry cleaners. The suits were like the man — basic and reliable and a little crinkled at the edges. He changed the shirts on a regular, well-pressed basis, and they looked at odds with the general rumple of his outfit.

"What was the call-in again?" Tru said as she pulled the unmarked car over to the curb and radioed their arrival at the location to the dispatcher. She looked at the building and unconsciously reached up to smooth a wave in her collar-length brown hair. Her deep-set dark gray eyes spanned the smoldering structure and narrowed in concentration.

"Came from some fire department investigator. Building burned late last night or early this morning, depending on your perspective. The arson investigator was apparently doing his standard once-over when he found the body," Garvan said, checking his notes.

"What's his name? Do we know this guy?" Tru wiped the remaining weariness from her eyes and was sorry she had missed her morning coffee. Having fallen out of bed, she'd had to compose herself before she could answer the phone call that had summoned her to the fire.

She had hoped that the call was from Marki. Things between them had gotten to that awkward, middle-path stage in a relationship. Under Marki's constant urging, Tru was beginning to feel the pull to commit more seriously or back off. She'd wanted to talk to Marki. But that was becoming more difficult. The Marki who was her lover was being confounded by the Marki who was the practicing psychologist. And that Marki had taken to analyzing every moment or falter in their relationship. The Ph.D. Marki was beginning to show up all too often and at awkward intimate moments. For Tru, the last two months had been more like antagonistic therapy than love and its customary affections.

Tru shook her head. She wanted to concentrate and focus on the tasks at hand. She had wanted to have time for coffee, a morning cigarette, and a little gentle conversation with Poupon, her cat. She had not been that lucky, and things didn't look as though they were going to change. Twenty minutes after taking the phone call from dispatch, she'd picked Garvan up at his house and cruised over the viaduct and into the West Bottoms.

"Never heard of him. C.D., or Seedy, something like that anyway," Garvan said, looking at the notepad and the pen scratches of his handwriting.

"Come on, let's go find him and see what he's got for us," Tru said, getting out of the car. She pulled her coat around her and strode purposefully across the street.

The air was beginning to brighten with the rising of the fall sun. The humidity-cooled winds sweeping across the river, flowing south across the Kansas side, made Tru pull up her coat collar and hold it tightly against her neck.

Tom Garvan watched the easy motion of her limbs carry her farther and farther from him. He held a personal prejudice that smaller persons were by nature more quick and agile than their larger counterparts. He felt a pang of envy as he watched the fluidity and potency of Tru's lithe, compact body. He would not ever mention his observations to her. Open personal gestures from him would have elicited a derisive response, and he did not want to hear that reproach in her voice. Worse, she might laugh at him wonderingly or eye him suspiciously and not laugh at all. Her moods had become mercurial lately, and he had no intention of getting sideways with her. He hoped that her atypical closed demeanor and seeming irritation with the world would go back to where it came from.

He tried running a few steps to catch up with her but gave it up for clumsy. She was talking with one of the uniform officers by the time he caught up to her.

"Officer, officer," an anxious male voice shouted in their direction.

"What?" Tru said, piqued as she turned away from her conversation with the officer. Her eyes narrowed as she watched a nattily dressed middle-aged man rapidly stride toward her.

The man stopped in front of Tru, towering over her. "Officer, I want to know what the hell is going on here!" The tilt of his chin wore the distinct impression of someone who was used to intimidating or impressing others.

Tru bit her tongue slightly in annoyance. She was caught between two choices of response. Bite her tongue or bite his head off. She chose diplomacy. "There's been a fire of apparently suspicious origins. That makes it a crime scene. Outside of that, I'm not sure I can help you." She turned her attention back to the officer.

"Look here, Missy . . ." the man's voice was going to the next stage of his intimidation technique.

"That's Detective North, mister."

"Detective North, then," the man breathed vehemently. "My name is Ronald Rinhart. I own this building and I want in. My offices are on the third floor. Its absolutely imperative that I find out what sort of damage has been done. And for your information, detective, I had dinner with the deputy mayor and finance officer last night. My friends might not be pleased to know about your attitude or that you're interfering with my business," Rinhart bellowed.

"Well," Tru said, trying to master her face and feeling her anger rise in her throat at his direct attempt to get his way by name-dropping. "I had no idea you owned this building. Neither did I realize that you knew the deputy mayor or anyone else for that matter. But I have heard that the deputy mayor's taste runs to the Mediterranean cuisine. I'm sure it was a lovely dinner. Dinner or no, this is an investigation. No one, I mean absolutely no one, is getting in here until I say so. That would include the deputy mayor. Say hello to her for me the next time you see her," Tru said as she turned back to resume her conversation with Tom and the securing officer.

"Detective North, I could have your badge," Rinhart fumed.

"You could, but why would you want it? There's no money in it and more recently not much satisfaction," Tru confessed. "I seem to be battling interference rather than getting on with productive investigations."

"Now see here —"

"Mr. Rinhart, if it is your building, then there is something you can do for me that would make it quicker and simpler for you to get inside. I'm sure we both have concerns about what happened here, but for different reasons. The longer you delay me, the longer it's going to take to get the fire department's and my reports to your insurance agent. I imagine that could cost you money."

"That's my point. What do you need from me?"

"I'd like for you to sign a consent to search. If I have that from you for those areas you control, like your office and any unrented floors or rooms, then I can get my work done more quickly. And the quicker I get done, the quicker you'll get back inside. Sound like a deal?" Tru nodded for Garvan to go to the car to retrieve a consent-to-search form from her brief-case. Garvan took his cue and jogged for all his weight would allow.

"Why do you need consent to search? Seems to me you've got half the town in there now." Rinhart's face screwed up in puzzlement.

"First responders and an arson investigator," Tru said as she turned back to the fuming man. "I'm not a first responder. It's a little detail thing for me. My way of covering all the bases. The officers inside are all with the fire department. The police department is here to assist them. And since you're here, I was hoping that in the interest of time and your concern for your property you might like to cooperate."

"It will speed things up?" Rinhart's fury seemed to dissipate under the hint of Tru's interest for his inconvenience.

"Yes, it will. A thorough investigation will still take time, but not as long as it would if I have to get a search warrant from a judge. I'm willing to do that, but it could take all day. Maybe longer. Whatever it takes, you won't be able to get back inside until I'm finished with everything I need to do," Tru said as Garvan jogged up beside her.

"Doesn't sound like I have much choice," Rinhart said, glaring at Tru.

"We always have choices. Maybe not good ones, but we have them just the same."

"Where's that damn piece of paper?"

"Here," she said, taking the form from Garvan. "Fill this out and the attached questionnaire. Give the consent back to the detective. I'll contact you later for the questionnaire. We'll expedite this for you as much as we can."

Rinhart took the forms and glanced over them. He didn't look happy at the extensive questionnaire.

Tru turned her back on him, winked at the securing officer, and walked into the interior of the burned building. She strolled to the midpoint of the lower floor until the dark shadows of the room hid her from observation on the street. Rinhart looked up, seemed to be searching the darkened interior of the building, and in frustration turned to Garvan who stood close by. She watched the pantomime between Tom and Rinhart. She saw Rinhart look again uncertainly into the building. She watched Rinhart's shoulders slump in resignation as he signed the consent form before handing it back to Tom.

She scrutinized his gestures as he flipped through the eight-page, hundred-forty-five-question document and waved it in exasperation. She noted how Rinhart looked behind him as a television camera-crew van pulled into the emergency-vehicle-congested street. He turned briskly on his heels and hurried toward his car.

Tom walked into the building. "Left me to the shark," Tom muttered at Tru.

"No, I didn't, he was going to sign anyway, but if I'd stood there he would have tried to ask a lot more questions and give me more of his bully bluster. I'm not in the mood for him or his kind right now. And I don't think it's time for questions from him right now. The other form will keep him busy and lock in whatever story he wants to tell. We'll get to him later. What I wanted was for him to see you as my second, someone with no answers, and I wanted those forms signed. We know you are none of those, but it's what he needed to think. We just team-played him. We got what we wanted. If he'd had too long to think about it, he might have refused. This way he thinks he's cooperating, because he is. No fuss, no muss."

"Do you think he's heard there's a body up there?" Tom asked, casting his eyes toward the stairway.

"No, but that is the point isn't it? I didn't notice him talking to any of the firefighters. Of course I didn't notice him that much until he jumped us. Everyone's a suspect at this point. It is handy knowing who owns the building. He will be a good source of background information when we get to that. If we need to get to that."

"A little shifty, aren't you?"

"Comes with the territory," Tru said as she turned toward the darkened stairs.

Tru and Tom worked their way through the rubble, carefully picking safe footing in the darkened building. They clambered slowly over the scorched debris, shattered glass, and charred loose timbers and went up to the sixth floor. The interior was very dark, damp, and cold. The flames and the heat had been extinguished over an hour ago, but in that closed charcoaled space, suggestions of heat lingered on the stairwells like a whispered threat. Windows that normally would have provided a flow of sunlight were covered in soot. They stood next to other windows with heat-shattered panes.

The interior was splintered with light and dark. The shadow of the rising bluffs still gripped the building in last darkness before morning. Tru and Tom made their cautious way up through hazardous footing and the noxious odors hanging in the air.

At the sixth-floor landing Tru heard voices with the undertones of a low contralto dominating the sounds. As she rounded the corner into the wide-open floor, she tripped over a stack of sodden ceiling tile and stumbled cursing into the room.

"What are you people doing here?" A woman's throaty voice demanded as Tru skidded on the tiles, struggling to keep her feet under her.

Managing to stay upright, Tru looked up to get a

fix on the location of the voice as the glare of a flashlight hit her square in the face, blinding her. It hit her like a hammer.

"Get that thing out of my face," Tru commanded. "I'm Detective North and this is Detective Garvan. I could ask what you are doing here."

"I'm the one who called you," C. B. replied.

"You're C. C.?" Tru asked as she and Garvan walked toward the sound of the woman's voice and the wavering light. She held her hand out in front of her face to ward off the offending light that continued to glare at her.

"That's C. B., C. B. Belpre. Arson Investigation Unit. The women and men with me are doing a little cleanup for hot spots. We have to make sure the fire is out. Don't want any members of the police department to go up in smoke." C. B. ground her teeth at the chill and challenge the detective brought in with her.

"This is arson?" Tru asked as she moved carefully toward the arching lights and sounds of the working firefighters.

"Actually, I don't know that yet. However, there is a dead body. That's why I called the police department. Policy says we're supposed to cooperate with each other in these things. By the way, do you always go stumbling around in the dark?" A hint of amusement leaked through the question.

"Yes," Tru responded curtly. "Learned it at the academy. It's a trade secret. Where's the body?"

"Well, if you can get here without injuring yourself, it's over where I'm standing. It's safest to walk directly toward my voice. There will be a load-bearing beam under your feet. It's best to just listen and walk where I tell you in case the floor's been undermined by fire."

"I hope no one's destroyed evidence while tidying up after the fire."

"We know what we're doing, detective," the arson investigator's voice said tightly.

"Sure you do," Tru responded faintly. Tru walked toward the light as it waltzed across the floor leading to the woman at the other end. For all her years in law enforcement with its policies, rules, regulations, and dictates, Tru's nature rankled under authority. The intimation in the woman's voice, the directive to follow her demands, and the assured confidence served to raise old habits of challenge in Tru.

Closer in, the light flickered up and over to the heat-seared body as it swayed above its contact with the floor. A short series of ropes, which disappeared upward into the gloom, suggested the termination of the fatal design. The face, or what was left of it, was hidden by a mask, a cooper-toothed zippered grin reflecting back at Tru.

"Great," Tru whispered hoarsely under her breath. "You got an extra flashlight?" Tru asked C. B.

"Right here," C. B. responded and handed the blunt end of a long flashlight to Tru.

Tru reached out into the shadowed space and felt the cold metal end slap solidly into the palm of her hand. It was an odd sensation of disembodied materialization. Tru shuddered in spite of herself.

C. B. watched the nattily-dressed detective walk a wide perimeter around the body and used her flashlight to reinforce the illumination the detective labored in. Watching the detective, C. B. shifted in her firefighter boots, thought about the practical work clothes she wore, and wondered if the detective ever looked less serious or more engaging.

Like other firefighters, C. B. didn't care too much for the police. It was no great secret that most firefighters viewed the police as privileged and pampered city employees. Apparently the cops got the headlines and firefighters got left with the dirty and dangerous work. Years of agency budget battles, each standing on different sides of budgetary machinations and competing for the same scant tax dollar, had created a wall that stood between. Organizational animosity and subtle hostility had a way of seeping over into contacts made with individuals of the opposing representation.

"Call the lab boys," Tru said, turning to Garvan. "Get a coroner, too. If there was ever an unattended death, this is."

"Doesn't take much to see we've got a wrongful death, now does it?" Garvan quipped.

"Jeez, you're quick," C. B. chided from the shadows.

"Could be homicide, suicide, or an accident," Tru corrected.

"Accident? Are you kidding? Whoever strung this guy up did it six ways to Sunday. You call that an accident?" C. B. rebutted.

"I call it a dead body. I do not call it anything else until I've finished the investigation. Haste makes waste of evidence and other efforts. Kinda like you not knowing if this is arson or not. Isn't it?"

"Now look —" C. B. began.

"Speaking of looking, Garvan, make sure you tell those folks to bring plenty of lighting equipment. It's blacker in here than the captain's soul," Tru said, ignoring the tentative assertion she'd heard from C. B.'s voice. "I'll stay with the arson investigator, C. G. Get on the horn and get them here soon. This place and those stale whiffs of fume are ruining my lungs as I speak." Tru coughed for emphasis.

"We're supposed to be cooperating here, detective," C. B. said, keeping her growing irritation under control and almost out of her voice. The shorter woman seemed to be taking over the case, and it wasn't something C. B. would let happen easily. She intended to keep a grip on those things that were her responsibilities.

"And we will, or should I say, we are. But I need to make sure certain things are done. Specific information has to be gathered. You're an investigator. I'm sure you can appreciate what I have to do, C. D.," she said as lightly as she could and squinted as the light continued to flicker in her face.

"An appreciation, I hope, goes both ways."

Tru tried to manage a tight smile rather than let her teeth grind together as they wanted to. She could not see again, not in that glare, and wondered if the arson investigator was doing it on purpose. The dark of the room and the blinding sweep of the flashlight's glare doubly blanked the other woman's body. Tru felt as though the light wanted to make hard points on C. B.'s side of the argument.

"So, C. C. —" Tru began.

"C. B., not C. C. and certainly not C. D. Do you have a problem with me, my name, or what?"

"Sorry, C. B. I'm a bit other focused, and that light is very distracting. I'd appreciate it if you'd get it out of my face. I honestly don't want to have to ask you again. I do have your name though. I can promise you that," Tru said, tapping the left lapel of her black double-breasted jacket and the tiny microphone clipped to it.

Tru habitually carried a tape recorder. It was part of the investigative ritual she'd formulated for herself — no notepads, her hands free, and the opportunity to record people's statements. It also let her quietly dictate her own observations and quips of curiosity as she wandered purposefully through a crime scene. Her practice had earned a reputation of being a little devious, obsessive-compulsive, and an amusing curiosity as she was constantly in quiet conversation with herself. She recorded the tiniest detail that caught her eye. Every gesture or idiosyncrasy she observed about anyone considered potential witness, suspect, or reluctant victim was accounted for.

When she did take out a notepad, it was for specific keynote recording, speculation, or the regurgitation of events analysis. As far as Tru was concerned, paper was for court presentation, investigative leads assessment lists, and memory joggers. Words, statements, hesitations, and the little lies or half-truths vocalized by persons involved in a criminal act whether victims, witnesses, or suspects were the province of her recorder.

Released from the glare of the arson investigator's light, Tru used her flashlight to look at the cross beams, ropes, knots, and loops of cord that secured the body. She noted the way they created and forced the angle on the suspended body. She studied the position of the victim's hands and the chest-crossing belt that held the body upright. She whispered into the recorder, making comments to herself that she intended to check with the pathologist during the autopsy. Tru's lips compressed into a thin line as she looked at the floor under the victim. In her mind, Tru sifted through training and reading-session information, process, and speculation to uncover the elemental details of the picture presented before her.

She reached inside her jacket and pulled a small knife from its holder behind her holster in her belt. She easily flipped open the blade with one hand and scraped at a residue she'd detected under the feet of the body. She looked at the tip of the four-inch blade, sat back on her heels, and let a small sigh escape her lips.

"Much wine had passed with grave discourse, Of he who fucks who, and who does worse," Tru muttered.

"What?" C. B. choked. She'd been watching the carefully choreographed movements of the detective with pleasure when Tru's recitation shook her from her reverie.

"Oh, sorry. It's from a poem. John Wilmot, Earl of Rochester, 1680. I talk to myself. Apparently sometimes a little too loudly. Pay no attention."

"What do you mean? Or do you always entertain yourself with sexual quips. Or, could it be deeper than that? Is there something titillating you find about investigating homicides?" C. B. asked pointedly.

"It means what it means. It's simply the first time the word *fuck* was ever used in the English language. There was a course I took a while back. I'm sorry if it offended your obvious sensitivities. I didn't intend to be overheard."

"You took a course in that kind of poetry?"

"No," Tru asserted slowly, her voice hinting a tightening edge as she wondered how she was going to get anything done if the arson investigator kept bothering her with questions. "With the FBI. Several courses, if you must know. Healthy and pathological eros maps, and the companion course, erotic paraphilia."

"You're kidding. They give courses on that? In the FBI?"

"That and more. See, people do stuff. Sometimes they commit homicides. I investigate homicides. The deeds people do to each other. That's some real basic, albeit unusual, people stuff. The courses were designed to provide information to help figure out how and why some people do what, accidentally or purposefully, to each other. Three weeks of erotica and eros."

"And the city paid for that, I suppose?" C. B. let her flashlight waver over the detective's face again.

"Quite a ride. But it wasn't fun and games. You should've seen the homework," Tru said and tossed a careless wink at C. B., hoping her flippancy would shock the woman into silence. She wanted to get back to her concentrated tasks again. Sparring with the arson investigator was becoming a bit intriguing, but it wasn't why she was there. She needed to establish a sense of the crime to get to the bottom of the case. She didn't want to have her attention divided.

C. B. stared at the detective with new questions lingering unspoken on her lips. She watched Tru make a series of quick notes on a pad and decided not to respond to the pushy detective from her gut level. There were things she wanted to know, but they could wait.

"I didn't expect a woman detective," C. B. said

finally as Tru knelt near the area below the body and concentrated on a particular tract of the floor.

A tired, wry grin spread slowly across Tru's face. "And you shouldn't expect one very often. There aren't that many of us. It's something of a boys' club. I imagine its the same way with the fire department." She wiped off her hands, and stood up to glance into the dark where she thought C. B. was located.

"Are you one of their pet projects or tokens?" C. B. asked.

"I do not believe you could find anyone in the department who would ever accuse her of being a pet. Her teeth are too sharp," Garvan responded when he saw a lethal glare flicker in Tru's eyes. He knew the constant questions from the arson investigator were beginning to ruin what little there had been in her mood.

"As for being a token, if you mean substantial, then the answer is yes. If you mean superficial, I think not. Let me say this, however, that just because I'm smiling doesn't mean I have a sense of humor," Tru said as she slowly turned back to her work.

"Touchy, aren't we?" C. B. prodded.

"You know" — a bored tone slipped through her demeanor as she stood up to flash straight white teeth at the sound of C. B.'s voice — "I'm not sure why you've got a burr up your butt. I don't know if it's me or if your mama didn't love you enough. Maybe the last person you bothered didn't kick your ass hard enough to make an impression. I really don't care. I do care about this investigation, as you should too. What say we help each other? Do it with a lot less chatter and a little less rancor? Hmm?"

C. B. watched as Tru exerted slow, controlled movements and drew herself up to her full height. It wasn't very far. The quick caustic nature of the remarks caught C. B. off guard and caused her to momentarily seethe at the impertinence of the woman.

Kick my ass? Did she threaten to kick my ass? Spicy bitch. I'd kick her ass, but there're better things I wouldn't mind doing to it. C. B.'s thoughts made her chuckle as she watched the five-feet-five, slight-built detective adjust her jaw. "You know you might be treading a dangerous line, detective," C. B. said cautioning the detective.

"I assure you, it wouldn't be the first time," Tru sighed. It had been a difficult morning, and C. B. wasn't helping. Tru started to walk over to where she suspected C. B. was standing. Tru intended to explain very precisely to her irritating companion that she needed to concentrate. She didn't know where the conversation was going to go with the arson investigator, and she didn't care. The sound of footfalls on the stairs halted her. She switched the beam of her flashlight toward the doorway. Tru watched as the lab techs and assistant pathologist struggled through the debris with their equipment.

"C. G., I've got other stuff to do. Maybe we can finish our little chat some other time," Tru said, smiling in relief. She turned on her heels and walked toward the crowd of waiting technicians.

"That's C. B., Ms. North."

"Of course you are," Tru said without turning around as she waved a hand back at C. B.

Chapter 4

While the detectives and laboratory technicians worked over the crime scene, C. B. Belpre worked her way through the three floors damaged by flames. She wanted to find the point of origin. She had not wasted her time waiting for the police detectives. Her backpack already held two rolls of film she'd exposed taking photographs of the victim and the interior of the room where he'd died. It took an additional four rolls photographing the exterior and interior of the floors where the fire had been contained. Photographs of the mingling crowd and curious made up the remainder of the snapshots she'd taken. A clipboard held the sketches she had made of the interiors of the warehouse. Several floors had held ancient officelike spaces, bathrooms, and storage areas. An examination of the third floor had even revealed a gaping, room-size, tumbler-lock safe.

The second floor and first floor appeared to have been recently occupied. Desks, chairs, filing cabinets, telephones, and computers were in place, although sooty from the fire and water-soaked by the earlier efforts of the firefighters. She retrieved business cards from several desks and pocketed them for later use because no owner or occupant of the structure would be allowed to reenter the building until the investigation was complete. She made a note to contact them when possible.

There was a lot to do, but then there always was. C. B. shook her head as she recalled the eight partially completed arson investigation reports sitting on her desk back at a station for Company 4 downtown. Two vehicle arsons, four torched buildings, and two accidental fires at businesses. There was always too much to do. Amateurs, kids, and slick willies with a penchant for trying to defraud insurance companies or satisfy another need kept her more than busy.

She had been a firefighter for twenty years in Kansas City, and had served as an arson investigator for the last five years after her accident. C. B. knew fire and its aftermath, and she knew the various motives and pathologies of persons who committed arson.

C. B. understood that most members of the public labored under one of several false impressions. The first wrongful impression widely held was that poor persons were to blame for most of the fires set in the United States. The second incorrect impression was that the mentally ill were to blame for most fires. That prejudice was generally compounded by the belief that the poor were always trying to torch themselves out of home or cars to bilk insurance companies. Neither assumption was correct. Training and experience had taught C. B. that many supposedly respectable and otherwise normal persons were routinely sentenced to long or lifelong prison terms for arson. Arson did not require a level of poverty. Nor did it have to be pathologically motivated. It did require a motive, but then motive varied from location to location and need to need.

C. B. knew most firefighters didn't care either way what the motive for a fire might be. It was not an issue of right or wrong or benefit or blame. She'd learned to care about cause and blame. They didn't care because they were generally up to their armpits in battling blazes, trying to stay alive, or trying to make sure that other people survived. It was one thing at a time, and survival preceded speculation.

Although motive might be the simple inner drive or impulse of a particular individual, it was the reason or incentive that an individual arsonist had for doing the act. The question of motivation was her province, her quest, and her incentive to unearth the truth. Motive was not willfulness, which came after and was conjunctive to the rationality of a particular arsonist.

As she examined the floors, she mentally ticked

off a list of the most commonly known reasons for arson: insurance fraud, organized crime, elimination of competition, demolition or rehabilitation scams, vanity, revenge, prejudice, crime concealment, suicide or its concealment, vandalism, terrorism, and psychological compulsion.

"Don't jump the gun," C. B. whispered to herself. *Other things cause fires, too.* She cautioned her thoughts. *Things like electrical, gas, heating plant, or furnace malfunctions. Issues of improper storage of combustibles, clandestine laboratories, renovation accidents and mishaps, lightning, and direct sunlight had to be checked. First eliminate the accidents and acts of nature and then move on to the problem of people.*

On the third floor, C. B. located what was left of an electrical service panel. Deep charring and rolling blisters were on the wood floor joists far above the panel and behind. The familiar V-shaped pattern of rising heat and flames marred the wall and restricted the scope of damage in the vicinity. This and the condition of the service panel pointed to the possibility of an accidental fire. The fire had spread up across the wall, going with the availability of airflow, through a false ceiling, across the solid ceiling and out into the hallway.

Debris from the false ceiling, old plaster, and papered wallboard had dropped into a pile of rubble below the destroyed electrical panel. C. B. photographed and sketched the area before beginning to carefully sift her way through the debris, layer by painstaking layer. She wanted to find out if the panel was where the lowest point of burning had occurred. It was important. The lowest point of burn in the room would very likely be the point of origin.

Vernon Little, assistant coroner, set up the standing lights in a wide circle around the body and attached them to the small power generator. Securing the electrical cords to the floor as best he could, he pulled the starter cord. The generator sprang to life, and the light panels flooded the warehouse floor in a bright piercing flood. Awash in stark clarity, the victim cast its shadow onto the wavering backwash. It appeared huge and distended against the soot-covered walls.

"I'd like to have a full set of photos of the room, detail on the knots, the victim, and the floor immediately beneath the victim. Then some shots from over by the door to where the body is hanging," Tru North said to the photography technician standing next to her. "See if you can get me some really clear shots of the ropes, knots, noose area, and that pulleylike contraption. Take all the knots up close and back far enough to show position on the body.

"I know you know how to do this, but I'm interested in making sure we have a complete record of the interrelationship of rope ties, knots, and securing," Tru told him.

"I'm not taking offense, detective. You know what you want; I'll see that you get it. Maybe even add a little of my own stuff to make sure you have everything you need," Clark responded.

"Thanks," Tru said.

Clark had never worked with the infamous Detective North before, but he was beginning to get a glimmer of why some police technicians called her Command-on-Wheels. It was one of the more polite comments he'd heard. What had sharply drawn his attention was the even tone she used with him, the way she stated fact and need in simple terms. She rarely gave bully mandates. She did not yell, scream, or curse like so many of the male detectives. They used their profanities to fill in the gaps their education had created. Their only means of communication. She said *please,* for crissake. In six years he had never heard anyone else say either *please* or *thank you* for anything.

Clark watched Tru momentarily and wondered if she had earned her reputation from the envious. Time would tell, he thought. He did not mind demanding crime-scene supervisors if they knew what they were doing.

"Let me know when you are done. I'll want the technicians to fix the position of all the knots and bind the ends before anyone cuts them. Can't have any frayed knots, can we?" Tru asked absently.

"Sure thing," Clark promised.

"Tru," Garvan began as he walked to where Tru stood watching the assistant coroner examine the body. "Got anything in mind for what we should do next?" Tru did not respond immediately. "Tru?" he asked. He noticed the way her eyes remained on the floor below the body. As he watched, a perpendicular crease of frown ran from the middle of her eyebrows pointing upward. She was concentrating so hard she seemed to have become lost to her surroundings.

Garvan reached out and touched her lightly on the sleeve.

"Yes," Tru said, turning to look at Garvan. She blinked and returned to the moment. "Garvan . . . this body is a little too odd, don't you think? I mean, doesn't it seem a bit over the top to you?"

"You mean because the guy's trussed up and left to broil like a roast on a spit?"

"Maybe. He picked a hell of a place to play, didn't he," Tru said speculatively.

"Play? You think he looks like he was playing?"

"No. Actually, I can't imagine why he or she would have chosen this place, other than the fact that it's remote."

"Suicide most likely. Pity, though. To think he went to all that trouble when he could have waited for the fire," Garvan stated flatly.

"It could be a suicide. A bit elaborate what with the rope, wet suit, and all. You know what I'm getting at. You have to have seen this sort of thing before. Fatal fantasies, autoerotic asphyxia. Or do you prefer the more vernacular . . . a fucked-up fable?"

"Language, language. What kind of books you been reading? Doesn't sound like your usual Great Moments in History. Does our benighted captain know you go in for stuff a lot kinkier than *The Battle of Waterloo*?" Garvan said, feigning alarm.

"Don't try to be funny with me. And you are on seriously shaky ground if you think you can threaten me with the captain. I can't imagine what it might be like to have to tell the captain about that three-day blue flu you had. And how it landed you at the Las Vegas 21 tables," Tru bantered. She'd grown used to working with Garvan over the last three months and preferred working with him over most of the other detectives in the division. He was capable, and Tru knew that his hangdog expression was a cover for a quick mind and an unusual love for animated verbal warfare.

"Now, Tru, I was just kidding —"

"Then you know exactly what I mean. We've seen or heard about this sort of thing before. Look at the body, all dressed and no place to go. That is the way they usually do it. Isn't it?" There was a time and a place for law enforcement banter, and a time for serious conversation. And serious was her current intent.

"I suppose," Garvan reflected.

"Most of these scenarios are dependent on a basic set of personally prescribed ritualistic behavior. If everything is under control, they live to fantasize again. The flaw, the fatal flaw, happens when one of their self-rescue devices fails. Their judgment and ability to control the fantasy fails. Sometimes an unexpected or unsuspected flaw occurs in their body, and it prevents them from saving themselves. Sometimes the best-laid plans of mice and erotica go astray. His bad luck, if it is a he, was messing around here while someone put a torch to the place."

"It's not really clear either way, is it?"

"Not by a long shot."

"Some people's kids," Garvan muttered.

"Yeah, some people's kids," Tru said. She raised her eyes into the gloom and wondered whose kid was swinging on those ropes. She wanted to know what had happened to leave their toes scraping on the floor while their knees dangled hopeless inches away from safety and life.

"Detective North," photographer Clark called out. "Have you found something?"

"Yeah, maybe. You'd better look at this."

Tru and Garvan walked over to a darkened corner of the room. The lighting stand's canopy barely reached the edges of their figures. Clark stood by a mound of rubble and pointed at it. "Looks like clothes, maybe. They look really scorched, but they might have belonged to that guy over there," Clark said. He gestured back toward the body in the room.

Tru pulled a pair of clear plastic gloves from her jacket pocket, squatted down, and carefully lifted the material. "Get me a couple of evidence bags, paper first, then a couple of those medium-size tin cans in the trunk of my car. If there is an accelerant on this stuff, I want to trap it for analysis," Tru said as she turned back the first layer of cloth. The progressive layers of debris revealed a light summer sweater, boxer shorts, a pair of black socks, and a pair of dark blue dress slacks neatly folded and rolled up. She folded open the slacks and checked the pockets. In the left hip pocket she found a wallet; she found a set of keys in the left front pocket. She turned and smiled up at Garvan.

"Clark, have the technicians put each item of clothing into a separate set of bags. I don't believe any of the other pockets have anything in them, but check them again for me to make sure." Tru turned and motioned for Garvan to follow her toward the array of lights. "Let's see what we have here."

"Don't you wish it were always this easy?" Garvan said as he watched Tru open the wallet and look for identification papers.

"Bingo," Tru exclaimed and held up the driver's license. A husky, freckle-faced Darrell S. Mawson grinned lopsidedly from the fused protective lamination of his Missouri driver's identification.

"Mr. Mawson lives or lived at 750 Walnut. That would put him in the River Quay district renovation complexes," Tru said as she handed the license to Garvan and continued to search through the wallet. "I've got fifty, sixty, seventy-two dollars in bills in here. There is also a list of phone numbers, some photographs of friends, and a receipt from a liquor store over in the River Market area."

"And keys," Garvan prompted.

"Yes, absolutely. A set of keys to a car. I think we ought to look for that car," Tru directed. "I'm betting he didn't walk the three miles over from the River Quay. It's probably close by."

"He looks like he could have used the exercise," Garvan remarked, squinting at the photograph.

"You're not a nice man," Tru admonished.

During the next hour, Tru and Garvan watched the technicians perform their tasks and directed attention to items and areas that caught their attention. They measured and sketched the area and conducted a hundred other necessary details.

"Well, they're about wrapped up here. The assistant's going to be taking the body to the pathologist. It's getting pretty late here. I think we've done everything we can. What do you want to do now?" Garvan asked Tru.

"Let's do the book until we know better. First, locate this guy's car and then his apartment. Then we do the rest of the legwork. Find the owners of

43

the building, businesses, employees, a list of frequenting transients in the area," Tru said as she turned to go.

"Is this a great job or what?" Garvan grumbled as he turned to walk out of the room with Tru.

On the third floor, near the wide hinge-sprung door leading into an expanse of open desk arrangements, Tru heard noises and remembered the arson investigator. There was the cooperation factor, she reminded herself, even if the woman didn't make a good first impression. Tru reluctantly sensed she would have to make an effort not to further damage already strained relationships with the investigator if she were to keep obliging associations between their respective agencies.

Tru squared her shoulders, signaled Garvan not to wait for her, and walked through the door toward the sounds of movement.

"Hello?" she called out as she stepped inside. Uncertain as to the structural trustworthiness, Tru gingerly picked her way across the floor. Light came through a series of shattered windowpanes. "Are you in here, Investigator Creedly? Hello!"

The shuffle and scuffing sounds stopped. Tru watched a shadow emerge from a small, anterior room and move in slow purposeful motion toward her. Dust and soot motes danced in the somber light as the dominating figure advanced. It was an eerie spectacle, and it made the hairs on Tru's neck stand up.

"C. B. The name, again, Detective North, is C. B. Belpre," the silhouetted figure commented.

"C. B.," Tru said, masking her initial dread in the

tones of chagrin as she looked up into C. B.'s charcoal-smeared face.

The soot had settled on the woman's cheeks and accentuated the light crease lines. The accent seemed to make her dark brown eyes dance in a corona of mirth. The strong features of the face were softened by the sweep of dark brown curls across her forehead. Tru noticed the way the hair touched the face and the earthy smile that danced across the woman's lips.

Tru felt her mouth go abruptly dry. She tried not to let her attention follow the long curve of the woman's neck. She tried not to look past the slight fullness of the lips and down the shoulders to the tension of breasts against the shirt. Tru attempted to stop her eyes as they reluctantly drifted away from those breasts to the flat of C. B.'s stomach. She couldn't stop her straying gaze as it made its way down to the faintly narrowing waist, and rested on the modest curves of C. B.'s hips. Tru's radar was on full alert, and warning bells hammered in her chest.

Tru knew she had not tried hard enough to avert her attention when she glanced back into the vivaciousness of C. B.'s eyes. They had been watching her indiscretion. Tru quickly feigned room-scanning scrutiny and cleared her throat.

"Tough working conditions. You been at this sort of thing long?" Tru asked in her best nonchalant voice.

"Depending on what you mean, most of my life," C. B. responded and let the allusion hang in the air between them. "Five years in arson investigation, but twenty years with the department all told. And you?

Have you been at this sort of thing very long?" C. B. asked as the contralto of her voice washed over Tru.

"Long enough," Tru coughed. "The reason . . . the reason I stopped was to tell you that the autopsy probably won't be happening for several days. Forensics has a bit of a backlog. I've got to talk to the pathologist and get a few other things in motion first. We can . . . should probably keep in touch to see where we are and what we need to do."

"To see what we should do? Sure. When and what would you suggest?" C. B. let a small astute smile touch the corners of her mouth. There was a spark or two here, she thought to herself, a bit more of a stirring and there might be a fire.

"You know your schedule better than I do, and I have no idea where the follow-up is going to take me. Why don't we leave it loose," Tru said, willing herself to try to speak slower. *An unbidden blush of lust and I can't talk at normal speed. Or make sense*, Tru swore silently at herself. *This is not the time or place for this. I have things to work out with Marki. Goddess, a simple encounter and zap, my libido goes into overdrive. Goddess, what is that about?!* Tru chastised herself. "Here's my card. It has my numbers on it. Do you have a card?" Tru squared her shoulders purposefully as if the motion would work the lapse of caution out of her demeanor.

"Yeah," C. B. said as she reached into her right hip pocket and pulled out a small, well-worn leather wallet. She dug around in it past the bills, crinkled receipts, and a crumpled grocery list until she located her business card. Before she handed the card to Tru, she took a pen from a shirt pocket and quickly scratched several other numbers on the back of the card. "My office number is on the front. The other two are for my car and home. The check mark shows the car phone. Make sure you call me if anything interesting comes up. No use in us duplicating efforts. I do want to be at the autopsy," C. B. said as she handed the card to Tru.

Tru nodded and accepted the card as her glance passed over the particularities of C. B.'s face again. A small voice in the back of her head told her to behave.

Tru considered the warning tone of the voice in her head and decided to heed it. *Don't be an idiot,* she cautioned herself. She decided she needed some breathing space. She nodded at C. B. and left the too-close-for-comfort vicinity of the arson investigator.

C. B. watched Tru make her way across the rubble-strewn floor and out the door. A hint of a smile spread over C. B.'s face as she replayed the searching eyes of the detective. She looked forward to receiving a call. She decided that if she did not get a call soon enough to suit her, she'd put in one of her own.

Chapter 5

"I'd say that the late Mr. Mawson owned a Ford," Tru remarked and tossed the key ring to Garvan.

Garvan caught the keys in mid-flight, looked at the ring and nodded. The key had FORD clearly stamped on it. "Great. How many of those do you think are parked in the square mile that makes up the West Bottoms?"

"Doesn't matter, does it? This is where the word *flatfoot* comes from. This boring block-by-block, step-by-step search is the root of investigations. Like it or not, it's what we need to do. Except we're going to drive in circles, ever increasing wider circles until we locate it. Stands to reason doesn't it that our Mr. Mawson probably didn't want to carry all that stuff for too far," Tru said as she got into the unmarked police car. "Most people I know won't walk around the block if they can drive. Of course, Mawson could have had that stuff set up for some time. That still does not mean he'd want to walk too far at night down around here. I know I wouldn't without my service weapon, leastways not this close to Halloween."

"Walking wouldn't be my first choice daylight or dark," Garvan said, looking around at the empty warehouses. The sagging facades and tired streets that made up that section of the West Bottoms didn't remind him of anything hospitable. The Bottoms were always in danger of rebounding and bottoming out simultaneously.

An hour elapsed as Tru drove through alleys and streets and beside railroad tracks looking for the car that matched the key. She and Garvan took turns getting out to try the vehicles they located in the increasingly larger and larger circle. At each stop Tru recorded the location of the vehicle on a street map, the license plate, and the vehicle description. The confusion and irritation of not quickly locating the car belonging to Mawson began to show on her face. She and Garvan had covered every street and alley near Genesse, Nero, Wyoming, and St. Louis Avenue. Not one door yielded to the turn of the key.

"So much for theories," Garvan offered weakly as

Tru pulled up to a dark blue Ford van on Union Avenue.

Tru's eyes cut to the look of perplexity Garvan had on his face and sighed. "It was, after all, only a theory. Odd though, isn't it? Either the guy walked, or he came by taxi or some other means. I don't know what. But it doesn't sit right. I'm concerned that I may have been a little hasty in my assumptions. There is something we're missing . . . I'm missing. What is it?" Tru said, glancing around, trying to put the pieces back together again.

"Unless you have any better idea. Let's finish this area and then do the stockyards, Kemper Arena, and American Royal area. If that fails, then we go over to state line and check on that side to the bend in the river. Before we go to Kansas, Dorothy," Tru quipped, "I think we ought to look at his apartment in the River Quay."

"As you wish," Tom said.

"Tell you what. I'll put in a call to a favorite judge and ask for a search warrant," Tru said as she grabbed the handset to the mobile phone.

"For the guy's apartment?"

"Yeah. Might save a little time and arguments from the landlord and such," Tru said as she punched numbers on the handset.

"You got someone who owes you favors?"

"Not exactly. But there are a couple of judges who have been impressed with my ability to tell the truth. Especially when I'm able to tell the truths that make me look less than perfect."

"You, less than perfect?" Tom chided.

"Only when it serves a higher good," Tru said laughingly and turned back to her phone call. A few minutes later she hung up the phone and hummed to herself.

"Got it?" Tom asked.

"In the bag. They'll fax a copy to us, or we can go by and get it. In the meantime let's cruise on over to the River Quay. I think we've run out of possible parking lots here. Guess we'd better put an APB out on Mawson's car too," Tru asserted.

"That would be a hell of a bad night, wouldn't it?" Tom said shaking his head.

"What do you mean?"

"Well, can you imagine it? Not only do you get killed or end up killing yourself, but someone steals your car too! That's what I call having a seriously bad day," Tom said and whistled under his breath.

"Frankly, Tom, I'm not sure how one compares with the other. Dying, particularly the way he did, well, that would have topped it for me," Tru said and glanced wonderingly at her partner.

"Yeah, well, it's all like love, luck, or gambling. Either you got it or you don't. And sometimes it just seems that for some people, when it goes wrong it goes wrong all the way."

His remark hit Tru like a blow to the solar plexus. *Is that what's happening to Marki and me?* she wondered. *Are we going wrong slowly but surely all the way? Could it be a simple glitch?* Tru shook her head, turned her attention back to the street, and tried to concentrate on getting them safely to the River Quay area.

The River Quay renovation district was in the heart of City Market. The area had been a city market for over a century and a half. It had served as a major market area long before there was anything but shanties, cold-water flats, storefronts, houses of pleasures or vices. The necessary levees had first appeared in the early 1800s. Before the close of the Civil War, modest rows of unprepossessing three- and four-story buildings sprang up. After the close of the war, at the beginnings of the western movement, and through the roaring 1890s, buildings of grander design lined the streets in classical facade and rustic stone.

The history of the area had been long and often fraught with natural and manufactured disasters. Flood, fire, economics, and the mob kept the area teetering on the brink of annihilation. In a lot of ways, it had a great deal in common with the Bottoms.

In the early 1970s developers — some, it was suggested, too heavily beholden to underworld thugs from the East Coast — tried to turn the tide. Businesses were carved out of what was left of the exuberant Victorian buildings that dotted the street and the handsome sandstone structures that seemed worth preserving. The Bottoms boomed. Bars of all flavors and delights, restaurants ranging from the simple to the exotic, and enthusiastic storefront entrepreneurs sprang up overnight. The bustle and the money bumped along together in an odd harmony for almost three years. Then the boom turned to blasts. Buildings exploded, fires flared mysteriously, and early morning gunfights terrorized the surprised city.

It had been a simple matter of miscalculated greed and avarice between competing "family" members. City Market and enterprises attached thereto were a nice pie, but the families didn't want to share it. The exploding bombs and razed buildings drove tourists, their money, and finally the businesses away from the River Quay and City Market. No one except the greedy mob members was surprised by the downturn of the short-lived prosperity.

The FBI arrived, and a long series of investigations, wiretaps, and snitch payoffs cornered the responsible parties. The culprits were tried, found guilty, and put in prison. But it was too late. Day-tripping tourists, night revelers, and sensible business partners had been frightened away. They stayed away until the late 1980s and then they were reluctant to do much more than put their toe into the notorious area.

City Market, a complex of one-story, buff-colored brick buildings was set in a U-shaped lot covering nearly a block of property. The installation of garage doors on the overhanging porches was a sensible modification and a bow to the frequently curious mix of daily weather in the region. Steel doors disappear in good weather and drop for more traditional store openings if the day goes sour.

In the off chance of clear warm days, the permanent renters find the large expanse filled to shoulder-rubbing capacity with traders, farmers, and niche retailers. The market offers its mix of wares ranging from live poultry, fresh baked breads, old books, incense, and stuffed animals to cabbage and green chilies pasta. The only mobs to be seen over the last ten years have been mostly honest citizens and visitors grabbing at their intended purchases. No one remembered or missed the other more brutal mob.

The River Quay Development Corporation,

bolstered by early successes in renovation, joined with the city in an ambitious ten-year project to create tony apartments and commercial spaces. At stake was the city's desire to draw people back into the floundering midtown section, the parts of the city that people are afraid to walk in after five o'clock any evening any time of the year. The river's edge and midtown were linked to and suffered from the flight of those who could move to the suburbs. Color was not a boundary in fear of crime and the desire for acceptable decent living environments.

Some of it was working. Early renovations in midtown and the river market area undertaken by the River Quay developers had begun to see some success. They concentrated their efforts on the young, upwardly mobile, and civic-minded and on those who didn't want to commute an hour or more to their jobs and moneyed institutions. They were beginning to find people who didn't worry about being able to take care of themselves and those who supported the bolstering of community policing in the renovation projects. It was young, yuppie, and campy to live in midtown and the River Quay. And so went the advertisements.

The parties were hot, the people interesting, unusual, or at the very least a bit arty. The city called to the revivalist spirit and enthusiastic spirit of those who tended to live for something other than the American-suburban dream.

People came to the River Quay to be a part of a vibrant, urban neighborhood in the existing river market, a multifaceted dream with space for living, working, shopping, recreation, gambling, tourism, and the arts.

As she drove along Main Street, Tru glanced around and wondered at the attractions. She found herself speculating about her apartment near the Westport district and began to compare it to the River Quay. She wondered what it would be like to browse the shops of crafters and artisans in the evenings. She considered what it would be like to walk under the juvenile trees lining the walks. To stop and eat at the eclectic mix of restaurants, or dance at one of the bars. She fancied what it might be like to meet other delights in the historic atmosphere of the River Quay.

"A loft apartment," Tru mused aloud.

"What?" Garvan said turning to Tru.

"A loft apartment. I was just wondering what it would be like to have a loft apartment here and wondering whether I could afford it," Tru admitted.

"Something wrong with where you're living now?"

"Maybe," Tru muttered. She turned the unmarked car into a public parking lot. "Listen, why don't we get something to eat over at that Papa Jacko's?" she said, pointing to the small Italian restaurant on the other side of the street. "We've got to wait for search warrant clearance anyway, so why don't we make ourselves comfortable in the meantime."

Lunch at Papa Jacko's was a silent affair. Tru pretended to scribble notes in a notepad while Tom seemed to try to eat his weight in spaghetti. Between the notes she jotted was the real purpose of her silence.

Marki invaded her thoughts. Lovely, long-legged, psychoanalytically minded Marki had been haunting her for weeks. They'd become lovers in the spring, and it had been as wonderful and fresh as any promise of spring could be. Six months. In six months they had shared a few adventures, more than a little passion, and had drifted toward a firmer relationship. Then suddenly, a month ago, Marki had said something to Tru that had put a pall over the relationship. *A question,* Tru mused, *a guileless, seemingly innocuous question, and I shattered like glass.*

"Tru," Marki began as she rolled over in the bed to snuggle closer and to touch Tru's face.

"Yeah," Tru sighed, still basking in the soft warmth of their lovemaking.

"Tru, dear, I was just wondering. Is this *love* or *lust?*" Marki asked.

"What?" Tru's eyes opened wide and searched for the meaning of the question in Marki's face.

"*Love* or *lust.* I've been wondering lately if what we're doing is love or lust. That is, I think I'm doing love, but I've got a sneaky feeling you're doing lust." Marki's words floated softly toward Tru, but the slight frown lines in Marki's forehead warned Tru of the crowded nature of the comment.

Tru's eyes flew open, and she raised herself up in the bed to look at Marki. "I'm not sure what you're getting at, and I'm not sure at all if I like where I think this is going."

"It's simple, really. We've been together for six months, right?"

"Yes," Tru said, remembering their meeting. It

had been at the Round Table Bar. She'd been drunk, and Marki had been there, warm, irresistible, and supporting, literally. It had been a wonder they hadn't been arrested for lewd and lascivious behavior. Then she'd found her again and realized that it hadn't been a drunken dream. Marki was real, lovely, caring, and the first right thing Tru had managed to do in a long time.

"In that time, in these last six months, there's been a lot that we have done together," Marki continued.

"Of course," Tru said as she reached out and touched the soft flesh of Marki's left breast.

Marki lifted Tru's fingers from her breast, kissed them, and held them against her cheek. "That's just it, my dear little detective. Most of what we do, is this. Oh, we talk, mostly about a case you're on or how my classes are going. Then we make love. Don't get me wrong. There's nothing wrong with making love. You are an inspiration. But then you go home," Marki concluded as she laid Tru's hand on the mattress between them.

"I have to go home sometime," Tru said, trying not to let the tones of defensiveness sneak into her voice.

"Every night, or every morning? And when you go, I find myself lying here wondering who you are, what you are, and what we'll ever be for each other."

"I'm not sure I'm following you. I mean, I'm here. I'm here as much as I can be. I have to work; you have to work. My goddess, I see you and am with you as much as I can be," Tru responded.

"No, actually I don't think that's the case at all. You're here as much as you want to be and not a tiny bit more," Marki corrected. She watched in sadness as Tru stared helplessly at her.

"Let me try to explain what I'm getting at," Marki offered.

"I wish you would," Tru said in growing alarm and annoyance. She sat up and pulled the hunter-green bedsheet over her breasts.

"Now don't get defensive," Marki cautioned.

"I'm not getting defensive," Tru retorted.

"Yes, you are. Pulling those covers up over yourself like that and crossing your arms across your chest is a very defensive signal," Marki explained.

"Oh, for goddess sake," Tru said in exasperation. "Psychologists think anything that they don't do themselves under the same circumstances is a defensive stance. And don't try to go pop psych on me."

"I'm not. It's an observation and an honest one, too. You do it or something like that every time I try to get closer to you than the surface of your skin," Marki asserted.

"So?"

"So, I know you in my bed. I know the ways you make love and the ways you like to be made love to. I know you like your job even though sometimes it doesn't seem to like you. I know your dedication and how good you are. I know you love me in your way, but your way has been keeping us at a distance. I want more."

"What more do you want," Tru said as the edge of anxiety cut a little deeper into her mind.

"I want to know more about you. Really," Marki

58

said almost laughing at the perplexed look on Tru's face. "Tru, sweetest, for all I know about you, you could have sprung from a seashell. I don't know who your parents are, where you went to school, if you have any siblings, if your people were good to you when you were growing up, when you first knew you were gay, why you were with that woman who didn't love you for so long, and what you dream of at night when you're not here. Tru, you've never told me any of those things."

"It just hasn't come up," Tru defended.

"Not come up? You're kidding, right?"

"No."

"Then on top of these little lapses of information, you've got a few lapses in memory. Why, just last week while we were at that concert in the park, I asked you if your parents were still alive and if they lived in Kansas City, Missouri. You never responded."

"Didn't I?"

"No, you did not. You turned to me, smiled sweetly, and asked me if you could go get me a Coke from one of the vendors. You evaded the question completely."

"I didn't intend to. I guess I hadn't heard you. I was probably listening to the music and just thought you might be thirsty. That's innocent enough, isn't it?" Tru objected.

"It wasn't the first time. It seems you have an interesting selective-hearing ability. I'm also beginning to wonder if you have some sort of deep-seated defense mechanism that keeps you from realizing what you are doing when you do it."

"Are you going to try to analyze me again? You know that makes me crazy. No pun intended, I assure you. Besides, you told me when we first met that you would be my lover not my shrink," Tru reminded Marki.

"That's true, I did. But that may have been a misstatement of mine. I'm particularly sensitive to your evasiveness because I love you, because I want to be with you, and because I want for us to live together. I would, however, like to know more about the woman who has so thoroughly captured my heart.

"I'm ready and I want to make a commitment to you. I just don't see how I can do that unless I know you. I can't know you, though, unless you're more willing to let me into your life." The last few words caught stingingly in her throat.

"Live together? Here?" Tru said, looking about the bedroom of Marki's house.

"And what's wrong with here?" Marki asked.

"Nothing. Your house is lovely, honestly," Tru candidly stated. The idea turned over in her mind. It was a lovely Tudor house. Native stone, small English garden with a hammock and patio at the rear. The graceful colors, hardwood floors, and comfortable furnishings that said Marki through and through were a great comfort to Tru. It was large enough to hold four large bedrooms, creative kitchen space, a living room with a fireplace, and an all but unused formal dining room. It was more room, ornately and tastefully appointed, than anything Tru had ever lived in. The house had been a haven of peace and comfort for Tru. It had been a focus of the love and sweet passions she felt for Marki. But she had never thought of it as becoming her home.

"Maybe that was the wrong question. Maybe I should have asked, 'What is wrong with me?' or

'What's wrong about the idea of us living together?' "
An edge of weariness and hurt leaked through
Marki's voice.

"I . . . I didn't mean . . ." Tru stumbled as the
phone near the bed rang.

"Hold that thought," Marki said as she answered
the phone. "Yes, you want to speak to whom? Oh,
yes, she's here somewhere. Let me see if I can find
her," Marki said as she cupped her hand over the
mouthpiece. "A detective Jones looking for you."

Tru held the phone to the count of twenty before
answering. "Yeah, Jones? Huh-uh. All right. In about
twenty minutes. See you then," Tru replied to the
questions from the other end of the line.

"You've go to go?" Marki said, slumping back
against the headboard of the bed.

"Yes. I'm sorry, Marki. Seems there has been a
domestic homicide over in the Paseo area. I've got to
get there," Tru said as she scrambled out of bed and
began grabbing at the clothes she'd tossed to the
floor earlier.

"Lucky you," Marki sighed.

"Don't be like that. I'll be back. This can't take
forever. We can talk some more then. OK?"

"It will take long enough and you know it. I've
got to go to a convention later this week. Chances
are I won't see you again until next week."

"Well, we'll talk then. I'll call you when you get
back," Tru said as she pulled her slacks on. "This is
a little delay; it doesn't change anything. You'll see,"
Tru said as she bent down and kissed Marki before
heading out the door.

Tru heard Marki grumble, "That's what I'm afraid
of."

That had been last week. Then Marki had called and told Tru that she was going to be gone longer than she'd intended. Marki said that her stepfather had become ill and that she was going home to be with her mother through the crisis. Marki had reminded her what she'd asked Tru to think about while she was gone. Left to her own devices, Tru studiously avoided the whole idea and hoped Marki would be in a different frame of mind when she returned.

Tru's cellular phone rang as she laid her napkin down on the table. "Hello," she said. A smile came back to her face. "Yes . . . yes . . . That would be great. Thank you, Judge. I appreciate your taking your time to do this. Yes. OK. Thanks again. Bye."

"We got it?"

"Sure do. If we need it with the apartment manager we can go back to pick it up. Signed, dated, and time logged. Let's get out of here."

"Are you seriously thinking about moving?" Tom Garvan asked Tru as he moved the lunch plate away from in front of him.

"Maybe a new apartment, a fresh start is what I need. No old baggage. Then I might have more room for myself and, you know, other things," Tru said as she put her money for the lunch on the table. It was the signal for Tom that it was time to go. Tom nodded and put his half of the lunch ticket on the table.

"Well, if it is something you want to do, as I understand it, there's one that has become available," Garvan suggested.

"What?" Tru said as they walked to the apartment building.

"Mawson. Mawson won't need his anymore. Maybe when the owners find out how he died, they'll give it to you cheap." Garvan shrugged and managed to keep a grin he was hiding from breaking out on his face.

"Nice man," Tru retorted as she glanced up the street and saw *750* on the side of building. She pulled the car to the curb.

Chapter 6

The apartment manager had wanted to see the search warrant. Fortunately, he was willing to settle for a faxed copy from the department, so Tru and Tom didn't have to drive back to headquarters. They did have to wait for the slow printing of the fax and the careful bespectacled reading of the warrant by the apartment manager.

"Satisfied, Mr. Humnell?" Tru inquired.

"Perfectly," Warren Humnell nodded. "Let me get the key for you."

"That won't be necessary. We have one. Thanks

anyway," Tom said as he and Tru turned to leave the manager's office.

"Well, then, I'll just take you on up," Humnell offered.

"That won't be necessary either, sir," Tru said, turning back to the apartment manager. "It's a crime scene, and for that reason, it is better that you stay down here. We wouldn't want your fingerprints to get confused with the murderer's, now would we?"

"No, we certainly wouldn't," Humnell agreed as his eyes went wide.

"After we finish, I don't want anyone — and I mean anyone — going in there. We'll put a DO NOT CROSS tape on the door. I'll call you and let you know when we release the room. And just for your information, anyone crossing that threshold without permission would be considered guilty of interfering with a police investigation. Are we clear?" Tru said, studying the man's face for understanding.

"Absolutely, detective," Humnell said as he sat back down at his desk.

Tru and Tom walked to the apartment elevator and waited for its return. Tom glanced askance in Tru's direction.

"A little hard on the fellow, weren't you?" Tom asked.

"Not really. He simply looked like the curious sort to me. I thought I'd square it so we wouldn't have anything to worry about later," Tru said as the elevator doors slid open.

"Well, it probably worked," Tom said as he shifted the evidence collection kit under his arm. "What the hell you got in here, anyway?"

"Oh, that? A little bit of everything," Tru said as

she helped Tom lift the heavy strap from his shoulder. "One step at a time and each step has a little point of deliberation to it. You know me well enough by now, don't you?"

"Sorta, but what I don't understand is why we don't get the lab folks over here to do this?"

"We will, but first I want a walk through without them. We'll make a few notes, and if we see anything we'll mark it for them later. I like to see a place before I have to compete for standing room."

"OK, but it's not the usual procedure."

"Not the usual case, either. Is it?"

"Guess not," Tom said. He watched Tru dig around in the case and come out with her video camera.

"All right. I'm going back to the end of the hall near the elevator. You stand on the other side of the door and try not to block any of my shots. Then when I get near the door, just open it for me. Use your gloves. I want to try to lift any prints from the doorknob or doorjamb that we can."

"Yes, your majesty."

"Stop it, Tom. If I don't do this the way I feel comfortable, I might miss something and you might miss it too. Then where would we be?"

"Pounding a beat again?"

"Yeah, but only if we were lucky," Tru laughed. "But you know how luck plays out with the captain. Distant and empty. For a career man, he's not exactly cop friendly."

"Hell, Tru, for a human being he's not *Homo sapiens* friendly."

"Right," Tru said, adjusting the light meter on the camera. "Get ready. Here we go," she said as she turned on the microphone at her collar and switched the camera to roll.

"October 25, 1:35 P.M., 750 Walnut, the hallway leading to loft apartment number five, belonging to deceased Darrell S. Mawson. Detective Tom Garvan and Tru North continuing the investigation of the unattended death of Mr. Mawson," Tru recited as she advanced down the corridor separating the two top-floor loft apartments. She approached the door and nodded at Tom. Tom reached out with his latex-covered hand, unlocked the door with the key found at the fire scene, and pushed the door open.

Carefully, with practiced slow, prolonged movements Tru let the camera cautiously record and sweep every room, fixture, and compartment in the loft. Doors, drawers, and closets were opened to reveal items hiding inside. There was no hurry. The eye of the camera had to review each item in every room with the same careful gaze of a human eye. Too fast a sweep, and detail would be lost or distinction would crumble into a wavering mass of fixtures without coherence. Tru took aim, knowing that the tape might be used later in court and viewed by a jury of tried, true, well-intended but unskilled citizens. She didn't want to operate the camera in such a way as to make them seasick from watching.

She noticed that Darrell S. Mawson had a discerning eye for air, art, and comfort. The loft apartment had provided him with a southern view of Kansas City. The skyscrapers, I-70 byway, and hint of the river could be glimpsed from large floor-to-ceiling windows in his living room and bedroom. No curtains, only stretch after stretch of wide, moss-green vertical blinds. The floors were a great expanse of blond tongue-and-groove wood with partial partitions designating the kitchen and bedrooms. Walls and ceilings were covered with the same deep-woods green, with the darker tint reserved for the ceiling. Strategically placed accent lights created halos in the kitchen, dining area, and living room conversation area and on sculptured art.

The sparse furniture added to the overall sense of space in the loft. The master bedroom was a bit of a surprise for Tru. The floor and colors were the same, but the style of decoration changed dramatically. In the bedroom, Mawson had chosen to use the large expanse to do triple duty. The formidable twenty-by-twenty room appeared to hold not only a lavishly festooned bed shaped like a giant sled, but a full Nautilus multifunction gym set and a computer work space in the other far corner. Where the outer rooms showed a firm nod to contemporary minimalism, the bedroom spoke of utility and a bit of clutter. Tru finished filming the loft and returned to the dining room area where she sat at the table and quickly sketched the layout.

"I'm done," Tru said as she set the video camera on the table. She turned away from where Tom was working and wandered over to the large windows overlooking the city. *This is a great apartment,* she thought. *I wonder if I could afford anything near as nice?*

She thought about her apartment on the second floor of a brick-and-native-stone post–World War II apartment complex. Her two-bedroom apartment had been built in the traditional shotgun approach so popular in that era. But it was home and, shotgun or not, the French doors in the living room opened out to a small veranda where she could spend late nights with Poupon, her cat, and a glass of wine. In the nine months since she had left Eleanor, she had managed to make the place livable. Eleanor had not made life livable, so Tru had fled Eleanor's house. *That was it, wasn't it?* she thought to herself. *It was Eleanor's house, with Eleanor's things, and Eleanor's rules. I was an interloper into her neat and tidy world. Owning nothing, being a part of nothing, except a respondent to her beck and call.*

The apartment in Westport was Tru's, although she'd barely laid claim to it through her sparse furnishings, which were moderately above garage-sale level. Books, clothes, a computer, and a cat made up her real life. No wall hangings or pictures. Few personal artifacts. Nothing that might give too much away or give too many hints of her interior identity.

Maybe if I had more space, I could find out what I like to have around me. Maybe I'd take a chance and create an atmosphere that spoke to me and made me comfortable. Maybe then the past wouldn't haunt me so. A half-mile to the west of her apartment, the state changed to Kansas and ran into the UK Medical Center where all the almost-doctors slaved out their residencies. She had moved out of desperation to get away from Eleanor, and it was where she had landed before she found or was found by Marki. She was as close to the Westport area as she could afford. She couldn't decide if she could afford to move in with Marki. But she didn't believe she could do that any more than she could afford to move into and live in the River Quay.

How would Marki respond if I turn down her

offer and move here instead? Would that be the last straw in the relationship? Could she give me space? Dare I insist?

"Do we know what this guy does?" Garvan said as he sat at the dining room table flipping open his sketch pad.

"Well, whatever he did, he made good money at it. These places don't come cheap. Not this sort of space. And not these types of trappings," Tru said. A frown crossed her face. She looked around the apartment and then wandered back into the bedroom to the phone by the computer desk. A list of speed-dial codes ran down the side of the phone. Third from the bottom, the word OFFICE appeared. Tru picked up the receiver and touched the button beside the number.

"City Finance Office. This is Loretta. Where might I direct your call?" a cheerful voice answered.

"Do you know a Darrell Mawson?"

"I'm sorry. Mr. Mawson isn't in today. Could I take a message?"

"Sure," Tru responded. "Would you tell him . . . you know, I can't remember his title. I want to make sure I have the right Mawson . . ." Tru said, waiting for the receptionist.

"Mr. Mawson is the deputy finance director. If you're calling about a loan, grant, or city financial assistance for community development, he'd be the one you should talk to," Loretta offered confidently.

"Bet he makes a killing on that," Tru proposed.

"Madam, no one working for the city makes much money. Trust me. Now, did you want to leave a message or would you like me to direct your call to someone else?"

"I'll call back later. Thank you." Tru hung up the phone and looked around the bedroom and the loft apartment again. She noted the decorations with a fresh eye for detail. She decided that for an underpaid city employee, Mawson seemed to be doing phenomenally well.

"Have you found anything interesting?" Tru asked as she walked across the room to where Tom dutifully sketched in his portfolio.

"No, not really. Guy seems to have been pretty much of a neat freak. That or he had someone come in and keep the place up for him."

"I imagine he had a cleaning crew. From all appearances, Mr. Mawson had enough money not to have to play the happy homemaker. I agree, though, he was fairly contained. Suits in the closet are organized by color, shirts have been pressed and starched by a dry cleaner, and his socks and underwear are folded and placed in tight little rows. Everything has a place, and everything is in its place. Makes me look like a world-class slob," Tru acknowledged.

"Makes my Martha look like a slob, and she has an almost intimate relationship with dust mops," Tom chuckled.

"Your Martha's a gem, and you know it. If she's so neat, why does she let you go out in suits that look like you've slept in them?"

"Is it that bad?" Tom said, looking at his rumpled jacket. "Well, OK, maybe a little. That wasn't my point anyway. Martha takes care of her job, the kids, and the house. I help, if I'm not off chasing bad guys. She simply lets me take care of my work clothes. Says she can raise the kids but doesn't think I can be cultivated much more."

"She may have a point," Tru agreed. "I never asked, but I was wondering . . . What made you decide to settle down and get married? Weren't you close to my age when you finally did it?" Tru asked, trying to pose the questions as openly as she could.

"Did it?"

"Yes, did it. What was it about Martha or, maybe more specifically, what was it about you that made you decide the person and the time were right?"

Tom Garvan put down his 0.5 mm mechanical pencil, looked slowly up into Tru's large gray eyes, and blinked in exaggerated surprise. "Detective North, you know it's those kinds of questions that raise more questions about the person who is asking them than the person they are being asked of. Why don't you tell me what is really on your mind?"

"Nothing. Silly curiosity. That's all."

"Right. So, Ms. North, are you in love or uncertain?"

"Love?! My questions don't have anything to do with love, or me, or me being in love. I was asking about you. I was trying to be conversant, that's all. We've been working together for months now, and I guess I thought it would be all right to ask." Tru felt herself mentally trying to leap out of the hole she was fast digging for herself.

"Sure, it's all right to ask. I'm surprised at the questions, however. You know, every time I've ever had anyone, man or woman, ask those kind of

72

questions, there's usually been a motive behind it. I'm guessing that your questioning comes from the personal side rather than some fascination you might have for my family life."

"Forget I asked," Tru asserted. She dismissed from her mind the idea of exploring the issues with Tom. "I've got to call the lab guys and see if they're through with the fire scene. I'd like them to come over here and see what they can find."

"Now, Tru, don't get huffy on me. You've never asked anything so personal before. It caught me by surprise. We can talk about it if you want," Tom said, trying to figure out how to get Tru to open up the door she'd slammed in his face.

"Nah," Tru said, dialing the cellular phone. "I was about to pry into something that wasn't my business. It's been a long day, and my mind must have slipped into neutral. Forget it. It didn't happen. I promise not to pry anymore."

"And you don't want me prying either? Is that it?"

Tru ignored him.

"Have it your way." Tom shrugged and returned to drawing and recording the measurements of the rooms in the loft.

"I'm going back to the bedroom and see if I can download the guy's computer while we wait for the lab folks. Maybe something in there will give us more insight into the guy. I mean, I don't get it," Tru puzzled.

"What do you mean?"

"Well, the guy was into a little personal bondage, you know. Hanging around, all those straps and ropes. From a textbook perspective, I expected to find more of that stuff here, and there's nothing. Not even the usual pornography, off-color books, or general fantasy material. Nothing. That doesn't add up for me. And for another thing, he was a city employee. Where'd he get his money?"

"Maybe he kept those things hidden. Particularly the leather and whips," Tom offered.

"That seems like a whole lot of trouble to me. I mean, when you want to, you want to. Period. Autoeroticism or plain old masturbation is a fairly spontaneous activity. Would you want to have to go to a U-STORE-EM or your friendly neighborhood bank safety deposit box to get the goodies? He certainly spent his money on this place. There was nothing cheap about his tastes," Tru said looking at Tom quizzically.

"Old money, good investments, a deceased uncle, perhaps. And for your information, Detective North, my wife would not let me have any toys or semblance of such things anywhere near our house. She's very straightlaced. She won't go to movies that have more than a rating of PG-13," Tom confided and winked.

"So, if that's the case, how did you have kids?" Tru laughed.

"Tossing and turning in my sleep, for all you need to know, young lady," Tom said feigning mock horror at her question.

"I stand corrected and apologetic," Tru said, raising her hands in surrender. Seriously, this guy's place doesn't fit the pattern. No artifacts, no rope scoring on the bed, no leather or lace in the wardrobe, and nothing about the gym indicates sex-friendly use."

"Well, there's bound to be something. And if there is, I'm sure you'll find it. Don't forget, this guy may have just got into this autoeroticism thing. Could be we're looking at an amateur. Could be it was his amateur status that killed him."

"Maybe. Would make for a hell of a situation. First night out in all his finery, goes too far and hangs himself instead of getting off, and the place he chooses to play goes up in fire and smoke. Make him one of the unluckiest stiffs around."

It was five o'clock in the afternoon before Tru, Tom, and the lab technicians finished with Mawson's loft apartment. They were bone tired and no closer to the reasons behind the dead Mawson than they had been in the morning.

"Let's call it a day," Tru suggested.

"Fine with me. I'd like to get home for once at a reasonable time to Martha and supper," Tom admitted.

"We'll start fresh in the morning. I'd like to catch up with the arson investigator and find out if she's fallen across anything we can use. I'll also call the pathologist and see when we can get the body scheduled for autopsy."

"You want me to check with the lab tech and see what they found or if they found anything?"

"Yes, that would be great. And, Tom, this thing is so thin right now, we can't afford to not look at anything, no matter how uninteresting, that might give us a handle on this case."

"Right."

* * * * *

After Tru dropped Tom off at his house, she drove to her apartment, had supper, showered, changed into jeans. By ten o'clock Tru had exchanged her unmarked unit for her own vehicle, pointed it in the general direction of the Round Table, the company of women, and a well-earned drink.

Chapter 7

Tru tugged at the heavy wooden door of the Round Table Bar and felt more than a little relief as the music and darkened interior washed over her. Thursday nights found the bar and its patrons gearing up for the long-awaited weekend. The backbeat undulated in the air as Tru give her three-dollar cover charge to the woman attending to the door. She smiled lightly at the woman and the memory of Marki the night they met six months ago. Her face flushed hot as the vision replayed in her head.

Tru shook her head and, with a conscious squaring of her shoulders, walked determinedly to the bar for the much desired beer. As she jostled for a place at the bar to catch the eye of a fast-moving bartender, Tru glanced around to see if any of the women near her looked familiar. As she let her eyes scan the women nearest and then out to the women in the darker corners of the room, she made sure that she maintained a slightly distracted look. She wasn't touring for flirtation, and she did not want to leave herself open to any advances. Tru knew she had her hands more than full with Marki with her ever-increasing hints at commitment and with the sudden new stirring she'd felt under the avid scrutiny of C. B. Belpre.

"Well, look what the cat dragged in," a voice behind the bar said.

"Better have been a damn big cat," Tru responded and turned her wide smile on her favorite bartender, Salena.

"I'm sure that it was. And just what are you doing here without that gorgeous hunk of woman of yours?" Salena said loudly over the crescendos of the jukebox.

"She's out of town till Sunday. I'm footloose, fancy-free, and in need of a cold draft. Any chance of getting served around here?" Tru shot back.

"Don't know. Depends. You two are still an item, right? You haven't gone and done anything silly, have you?"

"Not hardly. Not that it's any business of yours. She's at a convention or some such thing for professors. At least that's the story she told me. I've heard about conventions, though. Rumors and such.

All I know is that I've been left here to keep the home fires burning," Tru responded in the easy, quipping style that she employed with those she liked. And Tru had found Salena easy to like.

Salena had worked at the Round Table for three years. She had been promoted to bartender after putting in two years as a bar-back and then graduating from a city bartending school. Salena Partnoue attended the University of Missouri at Kansas City during the day to earn her degree in electrical engineering and tended bar at night to keep a roof over her head. At five-eight, she was slightly taller than Tru. She had long, rich dark brown hair, a square face, and an open smile. Although she was not a showstopper, it was hard to remember when her natural buoyancy and generous heart had not permeated the surroundings.

"Well, poor thing and thirsty too. What will it be?" Salena said, rubbing the counter in front of Tru.

"Just a draft. It's a school night. No more than three. I want to be able to drive home, and I have to be at work by eight tomorrow."

"One draft coming up," Salena said and moved back down the bar toward the beer tap.

Tru laid her money on the bar and turned around to watch three couples move to the music on the floor. She smiled at the dancers and noted that they possessed more enthusiasm than competence. *Much more interested in each other than the tune or rhythm.* She silently saluted the partners' best intentions.

"Are you a big tipper now, or is that the smallest you got?" Salena's voice rang behind her.

"What do you mean," Tru said as she turned to

pick up the draft Salena had set on the counter behind her.

"This is a fifty, dear," Salena said, raising her eyebrow. "I usually don't see these in here this far from payday."

"I thought that was a five. Let me have that and I'll give you a smaller bill," Tru said, reaching in her right hip pocket for her wallet.

"You thought it was a five? Jeez, Louise. Seems like you blink out if your girlfriend is not in town. Here, take this. I'm going to keep my eye on you. As drifty as you are, you could get in serious trouble tonight and not even know it," Salena said as she thrust the fifty-dollar bill back into Tru's waiting hand.

"Long day. Then again, most of them are. Besides, I'm a little old for a babysitter, and if there was going to be a babysitter based on age, that would be my job with you."

"I'm old enough to work here. Besides, I'm behind the bar, and that means I'm in charge. Marki would never forgive me if I let some big strong woman take you out of here and have her way with you," Salena protested.

"I'm perfectly capable of taking care of myself. And who says I wouldn't be capable of taking some big or small woman out of here and having my way with her myself?"

"Not a thing. That's my point. But Marki wouldn't be amused. She's not the sort of woman you should do that to. I don't think she'd take it kindly or let you get by with it. You two have been involved long enough not to want that to happen. Or is there something I've missed seeing when you've been in here together?" Salena said as she leaned over the bar to stare intently into Tru's eyes.

"No," Tru said, coughing nervously under the scrutiny of the young woman's gaze. "You haven't missed a thing."

"That's what I thought. I'll make sure I chase you out of here after you've had two. While you are here, I'll stand guard and do you both a favor," Salena announced and stood at attention. She grinned at Tru, who was shaking her head at the antics. Then she was distracted by a clamoring for beer at the far end of the bar. Tossing Tru a serious salute, she did a quick about-face and marched toward a frantically waving customer.

Salena had been good to her word to Tru. At exactly twelve-thirty she walked over to the barstool where Tru sat nursing her warm second beer and announced that it was time to go.

The two and a half hours that Tru had spent at the bar had seemed to fly. She had played four games of pool, the first three fairly well. She had managed to keep the table, earn a couple of free plays, and begin to feel sneakily superior in the game. However, the last game had been her undoing. The disaster had started early when the tall lanky woman dropped two solid colored balls on the break. It was downhill from there. By the time the game was over, Tru still had four striped balls on the table and the suspicion that she'd been hustled.

"Time to go," Salena asserted.

"No kidding."

"Yep. If you don't get going now, those tired eyes of your won't look any better in the morning," Salena said, sounding more like a den mother than a bartender.

"I'm on my way." Tru slipped off the stool to head toward the door.

"You miss her when she's gone, don't you?" Salena said as Tru walked through the thin crowd toward the door.

"Yes, I do. Yes . . . I do," Tru said without turning around.

As Tru walked toward her car in the darkened parking lot, she felt the pager on her belt near her left hip bounce in agitation.

Back inside the Round Table, Tru found a pay phone and called central dispatch. Five minutes later she dashed out of the bar and sprinted toward her car.

Chapter 8

There had been a time when twenty-three-year-old Jennie Dietz wasn't sure if life could get any harder and prayed that she'd never have to find out. She had run away from home and the sexual abuse of her stepfather when she was sixteen. Drifting from town to town, she had landed in Kansas City five years ago to practice the only skill she thought she had. Coming to the West Bottoms, Jennie could always count on a paying customer to provide her with a good meal at the Golden Bull Restaurant before compelling her to earn her keep.

Her raven hair, diminutive height, practiced wee breathless voice, and little-girl dark eyes had made her a favorite of the men who frequented the sporting events at the Kemper Arena. She knew she appealed to men who had a taste for children but not the indiscretion to actually accost one. Her customers could take her to dinner, pretend they were entertaining a young niece while in the public view, and then later play out their child molestation fantasies with an essentially clear conscience.

Shortly after her arrival in Kansas City, she had discovered the profit in allowing men to play out their forbidden fantasies. She had been standing on street corners in the downtown area near the convention center, sparring for space with the more established prostitutes. She had spent a month being threatened, kicked, and otherwise assaulted by the streetwalkers and their pimps for horning in on their territory. It had been a dangerous time. The threats and assaults were beginning to make her think about leaving the city or giving in to a pimp and letting him manage her action. She'd been desperate, hungry, and alone too long to continue.

The night things changed had been particularly harrowing. Several of the other women who were vying for the same trade had descended upon her, swinging their tiny but heavy purses about her head and shoulders. Curses, screams, and recriminations rained down on her as she cowered near a streetlight. People exiting the convention center hurried by, good family members refusing to acknowledge her or her assailants. The rain and the wind on that blustering night had seemed to side with the hookers and increased her torment.

Then a small miracle lifted her out of the fray. A long white limousine stopped in front of her, and a distinguished looking white man flew to her side, scattering the protesting hookers in his wake. He fairly picked her up and carried her back to the limo. Once inside, he briskly ordered the driver to head away from the vicinity of the rescue. For several blocks he simply held her against his chest and spoke in low quiet tones to her. He soothed away the fear, the bruised flesh, and the racing heart in her chest.

He told her that he had been watching her from a distance when he attended gatherings at the convention center. He said he knew she wasn't a child but had taken a kind of pity on her and her plight. He offered her a place to stay, a way to get on her feet, a warm bed, and some suggestions for her performance in her chosen trade. He had bought her clothes, sent her to beauticians, and coached her in the function and performance of her new role. He called her his child prodigy and she never called him anything other than Statesman. It was his joke he always told when he introduced her to his friends. And his friends paid well. Professional men, attorneys, politicians, CEOs and the like became her constant cash cows. He never took any money from her; he didn't need to. He had made his money years ago, and he now prided himself on his commercial version of Henry Higgins and Eliza Doolittle.

The money flowed in, and he became her Statesman. That's what she called him for his smooth deep voice, his elegantly handsome good looks, his air of moneyed refinement, and the genteel way he treated her. He was stately in his demeanor and charming in his persuasive techniques.

The Statesman's friends in high places were more than a little eager to pay five hundred or more for an evening with a clean, childlike woman who would fulfill their sexual fantasies. She had money in the bank, her own apartment, dreams of retiring and going to college. She was safe, as safe as she could be. She had gathered enough important, politically-connected names in her little red book to keep her in high finances and safely out of jail for the rest of her life. Life had been sweet except for the doing of the deeds. She managed her own affairs now. Her clientele were established, secure, and reliable. Even the Statesman could only count on her attentions every other week. But Jennie lived for the day when she could stop. When she could believe she had enough money, enough security sometime before her looks faded, and when she could leave the life for good.

Her customer that evening had dropped her back at the restaurant in the West Bottoms. It had been a simple job and wonderfully paid. Fifteen hundred dollars to let him pretend she was a twelve-year-old, eating a birthday cake while sitting on his lap so he could come in his pants. He'd been "daddy" giving presents to his little girl. Jennie had fought down her own memories and revulsion as she acted out the squalling delight of bouncing on his lap at the sight of the wrapped gifts he'd brought her.

As she waited on the street corner for the taxi she'd called from the restaurant, she promised herself a good long hot shower when she got home. Jennie glanced at her watch, ten-thirty, and she hoped her cab would be there any minute. She clutched her purse with the hundred-dollar bills nestled inside and tried to mentally hurry the taxi in her direction.

Suddenly, two buildings down and across the street from where she stood on Seventeenth and Wyoming, a small eruption and flash of light startled her. Jennie jumped at the noise and clasped her purse tighter. Her eyes darted in the direction of the flash and stared wonderingly at the building. It was the old American Royale Theater, a playhouse. Community productions and amateur comedy troupes had once occupied its nights. It had been closed for two years. The previous owner had a habit of putting most of the profits up his nose rather than into the business. She smiled to herself, remembering some of the amateur musicals she'd seen at the theater.

A twinkling orange glare danced in the basement windows as she stared. She looked harder, wondering if someone had tried to break into the building. As she watched, the orange lights grew and appeared to spread larger against the windows. Suddenly, a dark figure dashed up from the basement stairs and out to the street. Startled, Jennie slipped back away from the streetlight and stood in the darkened alcove of the restaurant. She studied the shadowy form as it ran north along the sidewalk past the cars parked silently beneath the streetlights. At the corner of Sixteenth and Wyoming, the figure halted, seemed uncertain, and then disappeared around the corner. Jennie's heart raced. She didn't like the feel the shadow-person had given her. She knew something was wrong and some mischief had been done. She simply didn't know what had been done.

She continued to look toward the corner of

Sixteenth and Wyoming long after the figure had vanished. She wanted to make sure that whoever it was, was gone. Then something caught at the corner of her eye, a cracking and popping sound panicked her, and she looked back at the building where the figure had emerged. Orange and blue flames leaped from the broken window of the basement of the old theater.

"Oh, my God!" Jennie exclaimed and ran back into the restaurant. She screamed at the hostess that she needed to call the fire department.

In the wake of the excitement and commotion at her words, Jennie returned outside after she made her call, found her taxi, and sped away into the night. The fire trucks arrived fifteen minutes later.

Fire Chief Daniel Flanders arrived with the first truck on the scene. With thirty years on the job, he was no longer aware of simultaneously sizing up the situation and issuing commands to control the scene. The sequence was automatic. Locate, confine, and extinguish were the rules that he and his firefighters lived by. As the first engine company on the scene, it was his responsibility to make sure his squad located the exact place of the fire before he committed his or any other responder to the block.

The American Royale Theater had been easy to find. It wasn't always a sure bet that the reported address would send a company to the right location. Addresses and actual locations could be confusing. Callers to dispatch central were generally excited and fearful, and they sometimes intentionally misdirected fire fighting response. It wasn't unusual to have an engine respond to a fire only to find that they'd been sent to the street address at the rear of a building instead of to the main street address at the front.

Chief Flanders was from the old school, and he had trained his firefighters to be the same. As a philosophy, the old school insisted that the first and foremost action to take after locating a fire is to confine the fire. It was a simple philosophy based on a simple set of facts, that fire has only six possible directions to spread: up, down, front, rear, left, and right. Flanders was aware that some of the newer commanders were inclined to protect the exposures of adjacent buildings from spread. But to him, that was both simpleminded and redundant. Protecting an exposure, for Flanders, was a good idea based on wrongheaded simplest terms. There were plenty of instances in which confining a fire within the fire buildings was of greater importance than protecting anything standing next to it. That the total loss of a building and the potential loss of life far outweighed the total value of a building was the one constant and generally applicable rule. It was a simple matter for Flanders that the rate of fire spread in most buildings was far faster than the rate of fire spread from the outside of the building to others. At a glance, the theater was a classic case of contain and extinguish.

Flanders directed the first engine to stretch a line toward the outside basement entrance area, where it was showing heavy fire. As the second engine arrived, he spoke quickly to the captain and directed him to have his firefighters direct their line toward the first floor of the structure. The captain and other firefighters would not be happy at his direction. They would want to get their "share of the fire," but he needed them to cover the open stairway coming up from the basement and to keep the fire from extending horizontally throughout the building. Containment was first.

C. B. Belpre arrived twenty minutes after the first call came in. She wheeled the arson van into the parking lot of the Golden Bull Restaurant, grabbed her video camera, and walked toward the side of the street where the engine companies waged their war against the subsiding inferno.

She let her camera pan the crowd standing in front of the restaurant. With her eye on their faces as she adjusted the zoom in and out, she chuckled as she watched the well-heeled patrons shiver from the cold October breeze and from their own excitement. She filmed the flames and the smoke that were ravaging the basement and first floor of the old theater.

C. B. lowered her video camera and sighed heavily, knowing it was going to be the second long night in a row for her. She slung the camera strap around her shoulder and made her way toward the huddled knot of transfixed onlookers at the restaurant door.

The gawkers paid no attention to her approach. The sights and sounds of the fire and of the engine companies locked in their deadly dual mesmerized them. She heard murmurings, excited whispers, exclamations, and gasps as the crowd observed the orchestrated frenzy across the street.

Central dispatch had told her that the fire call had originated from an anonymous party in the restaurant. *Anonymous* could mean anything — a patron, a porter, a dishwasher, or a waiter. C. B. needed to find out who had called, what they had seen, and the detail of the event that dispatch only hinted to. From the recorded emergency call, dispatch had told C. B. that the caller was a woman, her voice clear, firm, and articulate. The 911 center's caller-identification computer had revealed the address, business name, and phone number of the fire call. The answering dispatcher had completed the printout of the location almost before the woman gave her statements of observation over the phone.

The woman told the dispatcher, "There's a fire at the American Royale Theater. In the basement. A man, or someone, ran from there. Probably a derelict, and it seems that there might have been an explosion. Then he ran away." When the dispatcher had asked the woman to wait for the firefighters to give them more information, she had refused.

"No," she'd said. "I've done all I intend to by letting you know there's a fire. You can take care of the rest." And then she'd hung up abruptly.

Inside the Golden Bull, C. B. scanned the room and wondered if she would be able to film the patrons who had remained at their tables. She began to lift the camcorder's lens to her face when she heard a voice at her shoulder.

"Is there something I might do for you, madam?"

C. B. turned to look at the elegant hostess standing next to her. "Yes, as a matter of fact. You can do something for me. Which one of these folks called the fire department? I'm conducting an investigation, so I need to know," C. B. explained.

"What do you mean?" the woman said, lifting her nose ever so slightly at C. B. with an air of disdain.

"Which one of your guests called the fire department to report the fire at the building across the street," C. B. said as she flashed her arson investigation badge and identification at the haute young woman. "Is that plain enough?"

"Oh, I had no idea," the woman said as her eyes widened in surprise.

"You don't know who called?"

"Oh, that. No, I meant I didn't realize there was an investigation. I'm sorry. I simply don't know how all that works . . ." the woman said hesitantly. She looked C. B. over with care.

"So, what is it? Do you know who called? Is she still here? Can you point her out or identify her for me?" C. B. prodded.

"She left right after she called."

"And . . . ?"

"And, what?"

"And do you know who it was?"

"Oh, that. Not really," the woman said and seemed to fidget in her body-clinging gown.

"It seems to me that you are being very evasive, Miss. Perhaps you don't know the penalties for interfering or withholding information in an investigation? Do you think a night or two in jail would help loosen or refresh your memory?" C. B. threatened and let a smile slide menacingly across her face. She watched as the woman's shock and surprise fluttered in her hands.

"Oh, dear. I . . . it's just that . . . well, she's a regular, but she's rather *ir*regular. So I . . ." the woman faltered.

"Regular but irregular? Could you be any more

obtuse?" C. B. said, trying to nudge the woman toward a level of clarity.

The hostess leaned confidingly toward C. B., and in a low voice she whispered, "She's, or rather I've been told, she's a hooker. Comes here every two or three nights. Mostly with a new client. That's what they call them, isn't it? She can't be more than fifteen or sixteen. It seems a pity, actually," the woman said. She stood back and waited for C. B.'s reaction.

"A fifteen-year-old hooker called in the fire?"

"Exactly."

"Well, she did the right thing. But my real question is, do you know who she is?"

"I certainly don't know those type of people," the hostess said, looking shocked at what she considered C. B.'s suggestion.

"No, of course you don't. But do you know her name?"

"Ah! I once heard one of the men she was with call her Bo Peep, but I think he was trying to be cute. Then later he used another name. It sounded real," the hostess said, wrinkling up her nose. "I think he called her Ms. Dietz."

"Dietz," C. B. repeated as she jotted the name in her notepad. "Anything else? Do you know anything more about her?"

"Nothing other than that she had already called a cab and it picked her up right after she called the fire department."

"What cab company. What time was that?"

"Yellow Zephyr Company somewhere around ten-thirty," the hostess advised.

"OK. I may be back later. There's a chance you might be contacted by the police, too," C. B. said. She spent a few more minutes with the hostess getting the names of waitpersons, cooks, and other staff before she left.

Back on the street near the thinning crowd of onlookers C. B. made a note to herself to get the printout of Yellow Zephyr for the cab that had taken the fire-reporter from the Golden Bull. She decided she'd follow up the home address of the mysterious Bo Peep hooker and otherwise faithful citizen after she finished with the required arson check of the building. Next to the name Bo Peep Dietz, C. B. wrote "the sound of an explosion." She had a few questions for Bo Peep and wondered about the young woman's involvement in the fire.

It was one in the morning before the fire was extinguished and C. B. was allowed to take her equipment into the damaged structure of the theater. Halogen light in hand, she struggled across the wet, sooty floor of the basement. In the light of the heavy-duty flashlight, she let the beam scour the walls until it came to rest on the second erupted electrical panel she'd seen in less than two days.

"Now that's unusual," C. B. muttered.

Chapter 9

Tru didn't waste time going back to her apartment to retrieve her unmarked detective's vehicle. The message had been clear and imploring. "Meet arson investigator C. B. Belpre at the site of an arson and do it now." The dispatcher inferred that the arson investigator had indicated that the evening's fire and the homicide from the previous night might be connected.

Tru turned onto the Twelfth Street Viaduct, reached over into the glove compartment and pulled out a tube of mint-flavored toothpaste. She squirted a lump into her mouth and swished it around. She didn't want to show up at a crime scene with the smell of alcohol on her breath. She was relieved that Salena had played mother hen with her at the bar. Tru choked down the toothpaste and felt her throat constricting on the gluey substance. It almost made her gag.

"Long day and longer night," Tru murmured to herself as she turned down the off-ramp onto Wyoming Street. Five blocks later she pulled to the curb north of the dark-shattering strobes of the emergency lights of the fire engines parked at the smoldering American Royale Theater. Before she got out of her car, Tru checked her breath by raising her hand toward her face and blowing her breath into her palm. The sweet aroma of mint met her nose but she decided that having one of the ten cigarettes she allowed herself a day would provide additional coverage and assurance for her.

Tru walked toward the fire engines and the firefighters working diligently to drape and refold the hoses they'd used to fight the blaze. A breeze danced lightly down the street, and the chill in the night air made her pull her jacket more securely around her.

I'm not dressed for this. Again, Tru thought, ruefully remembering her concern for her clothes at the last fire. She had no such concern for the durability of the clothes this time. The jeans, shirt, and light leather jacket that made up her wardrobe for a night at the bar were wrong for working in the cool October night air. She had gotten dressed not intending to be outside any longer than it took to go from her car to the bar and back again. The humid chill seeped next to her skin.

"Can I help you?" a man wearing firefighter regalia and CAPTAIN emblazoned on his cap asked as he approached Tru.

"I'm looking for C. B. Belpre, the arson investigator," Tru said as she pulled her wallet from her pocket and flashed her gold detective's badge at him. She tried not to shiver when a gust of wind whipped at her clothes.

"Oh, yeah. She's in the building. Just go on down those front steps and take a left at the end of a hall. In the basement. Just yell at her. She's expecting you," he said and went back to helping his staff rerig their truck. She looked after him, envying his heavy firefighter's coat.

Tru stared at the dark, water-drenched building, sighed heavily, and resigned herself to her fate. The streetlights were not much help. They washed the street with shades of silvery gray, neutral gray, and more gray. She picked her way carefully across the tangle of hoses and debris toward the exterior basement steps. The stairway opened like a crater and swallowed the light above. It was worse inside the basement passage. It was as dark as a well, and she muttered at herself for forgetting to bring a flashlight. Tru squinted into the darkness as though by staring harder at the inky blackness she might give it illumination.

"Shit," Tru breathed and stumbled along the wall toward what she hoped was the immediate left turn the captain had told her about. She ran her hand along the wall and felt the crust of soot and water squish beneath her fingers. Suddenly, her hand shot farther into space and darkness before her. She momentarily lost her balance and felt her right foot unexpectedly slam down on another set of stairs leading downward.

There had been no time to even cry out. A sharp pain sprang up her leg from the jarred ankle, and she cursed under her breath.

"Break my neck, for sure," Tru whispered in aggravation. She let her left leg slide carefully forward and tested the width of the stairs. Air met the questing reach of her toe, and she slid her heel over the end of the step. Carefully she let the heel slide down the back of the step until she felt the sole of her shoe touch the next step. She continued her slow advance down to the basement. A tiny eternity and four stair steps later she felt the solid level of an open corridor.

Tru stopped and tried to let the pounding of her heart subside in her ears. She took out her cigarette lighter and peered down the corridor, wondering if she'd missed C. B. *Surely the woman's got a flashlight. We can't both go stumbling around in this obscure mess.*

"Can black get blacker?" Tru wondered aloud as her lighter glare dwindled and the darkness pressed in on her. She snapped off the lighter, lifted the remaining ember of her cigarette to her lips, and sought small comfort there.

"Not really."

The voice out of the dark seemed to roar at Tru and made her heart thunder in her ears. She gasped.

Her forgotten cigarette fell from her fingertips and was extinguished in the pooled water at her feet.

"Son of a bitch," Tru exclaimed.

"No, not at all," C. B. said, trying to keep a snicker from escaping her lips. She hadn't intended to scare the detective. She had simply intended to respond to her question.

"What the hell are you doing standing in the dark?" Tru exploded.

"I might ask you the same thing. At least I brought a flashlight with me," C. B. asserted.

"Is that so. Then, I repeat. What the hell are you doing standing in the dark? Shit, I could have shot you."

"Not as long as you were holding that lighter or cigarette. I saw the glow. I bet you smoke with the same hand you use for your weapon," C. B. quizzed.

"Yeah. So, what's your answer."

"I did bring a flashlight. But things happen. Like a few minutes before you got here, the damn battery ran down. Poor planning on my part, but at least I had one. I have a spare in the truck. I was on my way to get it when I heard you stumbling on the stairs."

"Why didn't you let me know you were down here?"

"Actually, I was afraid to say anything. I remember the way you were stumbling around yesterday. I thought it would be better if I waited here. Actually, I was concerned about your gun. I figured that if you were stumbling around with it in your hand and I said anything, you might really have taken a shot at me."

"So you waited till I was standing in the dark to announce yourself?" Tru asked as the anger continued to broil inside her. She hated to be embarrassed and hated the idea of looking like a fool, even in the dark when no one could see her.

"I took a chance, as I told you," C. B. said slowly. "I took a chance that when I saw the cigarette glow go up to your mouth that you were using your strong hand. Your shooting hand. That I might be safe for a second or two, and I let you know I was here."

"Fine. Whatever. You going to go get that extra battery or stand there and continue to amuse yourself at my expense for the rest of the night?"

"I'm on my way, even as we speak," C. B. said. She stood and walked toward the sound of the detective's voice.

Tru listened to the slow footsteps approach her. She felt the brush of the woman's clothes against her and the touch of a hand on her arm as C. B. walked past her and up the stairs.

"This shouldn't take very long," C. B. said from somewhere in the dark above Tru.

Tru stood at the bottom of the stairs. The hair on her neck slowly rose and tickled her subconscious. Tiny little alarm bells clanged in a distant corner of her mind. The images of the dream she'd had began to emerge in too great a clarity as the basement walls pressed in. It breathed. The steady dripping of water from the ruined ceiling fell on her head, splashed in invisible pools around her feet, and mixed with the acidic smell of charred wood and roasted cement. Something stared, grew, and inhaled beyond her.

Tru reached for the two-inch stubby .357 on her belt. Her hand slid to the butt of the gun, and her thumb released the safety. She slid the gun slowly out of its holster till it rested firmly in her hand and was pointed at the distance in front of her down the corridor.

"Only a dream," she whispered to herself and waited to see if the dream would reveal itself in the black, burned-out basement.

"OK," C. B.'s voice rang out on the steps behind her. "This will work," C. B. said as she shone the light on the steps in front of her and walked nonchalantly down the stairs.

Tru felt, saw, the bright sweep of the flashlight as it hit her back and cast her long shadow into the basement expanse. The growing light secured the basement, vanishing the shadow-in-shadow, and the nightmare retreated.

"I'll show you what I've found," C. B. said, standing a breath away from Tru. "Come, I'll show you." She reached out and put her hand on Tru's shoulder and turned away, brushing slowly against Tru in the narrow confines of the hall.

Tru felt her body tingle at the feeling of the brief contact with C. B. Tru followed haltingly. Her nerve endings were on full alert after her unhappy encounter with her imagination. Her present overactive suggestibility contrived to play images of her hands exploring C. B.'s breasts and down to the curve of her hips. The idea played in her head and let her imagination explore the tantalizing possibilities until she stubbed her toe on a packing crate.

"Ouch," she mumbled, more in irritation than pain.

"Are you coming all right back there?" C. B.'s voice shot through the dark.

"Yeah. Fine. You could share that light a little more," Tru suggested as she watched the retreating figure turn a corner and vanish. *I could keep my mind on business too,* Tru thought ruefully.

She tried to follow C. B.'s retreating back through the elongated basement. The woman's long legs and certainty of step in the circle of light did not help Tru as she tried to maintain her footing on the rubble-strewn floor. Tru stumbled a couple of times, bit her tongue to keep herself from cursing aloud, and slugged toward the receding glare of the light. She didn't want C. B. to hear her complain again. The woman was irritating, and Tru didn't want C. B. to think of her as a stumbling, bumbling fool. *Crap, what do I care what she thinks?* Tru queried in her irritated mind.

The light returned and flicked momentarily in Tru's face. She heard the sound of C. B.'s feet move back toward her down the corridor. C. B. walked steadily toward Tru and stopped in front of her.

"You know, you've got a good idea there. Sharing the light would be a bit more polite than running off and leaving you back here in the dark," C. B. commented. "I usually work alone, and I guess it's an inappropriate tendency to act that way when someone else is around."

"Apology accepted," Tru said and felt herself take

a silent quick intake of air as she felt C. B.'s hand reach out of the darkness to grip her shoulder. C. B. let her hand slide down Tru's arm until she'd tucked her elbow in close to her side.

"Come. I'll take you where we need to go."

The frosty October air swept through the fire-shattered windows and swirled down into the basement room. The mingling of fall air and the permeating moisture nipped at the women. They walked along the close dark hallway arm-in-arm until they emerged into a wide open floor space where street-level windows offered slanted light. C. B. moved her hand from Tru's arm and then held her hand. She nodded in the appropriate direction and pointed the beam of the flashlight.

"It's over here," C. B. said. She let her hand fall from Tru's to immediately rest lightly on the small of her back. "I might have missed this again. Lucky I didn't."

"Beg pardon?" Tru said in distraction. From where C. B.'s hand touched her, a mischievous fever burned up her back, across her shoulders, and along the skin of her arms.

"If I hadn't heard a replay of the 911 call, I meant. I listened to a recording of the 911 fire report. The caller said she'd seen a flash of light followed by a bursting noise, or something like that. Then she said she saw a person running from the building. Anyway, it got me to thinking. One thing can suggest another, if you're paying attention. You know how that is," C. B. said, turning her head toward Tru.

"I do," Tru said as a whisper of C. B.'s breath touched her cheek.

"Really? Then you're familiar with electrical fires?"

"Ah, no, not really."

"But I thought you said . . . I see. Aren't we talking about the same things?"

"Of course we are. But tell me what I'm supposed to be looking at," Tru breathed as she tried to shake captivating vignettes from her mind.

"It's safe. We're in no danger. I made sure the electrical meter was disconnected. We won't get electrocuted," C. B. said as she guided Tru toward a far wall. "While I was waiting for you and before my other flashlight burned out, I checked the rating of the fuses, the gauge of wire, the rating of the service panel, and the total load potential of the unit. I wanted to make sure of the basics and find out if this unit was in compliance with code."

"OK," Tru said, trying to sound interested and make sense out of why those things might be important. The constant contact of C. B.'s hand on her back and at her waist as she gave her technical discussion didn't help.

"Everything checked out. Just like it did in the building yesterday. See, this fire and the other one seem to have originated in the service panel. That happens sometimes. But usually there's been some tampering, where someone has gone in and jury-rigged the thing. Meaning they didn't have it UL approved, or they didn't account for an increase in electrical load when it was converted from fuses to circuit breakers. That sort of thing is usually done by lazy contractors or by idiots who don't know they can kill themselves with their tinkering. Anyway, since it wasn't out of code, and I couldn't see any tampering,

I only saw what I expected to see, or what someone wanted me to find and conclude."

"How's that?"

"When you have a fire in a fuse box or service panel, it's usually accompanied by a detonation. When that happens, the door or cover blows off too. It did here, and it did in the other fire. The explosion happens because the supply lines, like those" — C. B. directed her flashlight glare to the thick electrical cables dangling around the service panel — "come into the service panel, here and here." She pointed with her index finger to the electrical junctures. "When those two opposing potentials make contact with each other, a violent explosion can happen. When the explosion occurs, the fire inside the panel box blows the lid off and the fire escapes into the rest of the area surrounding the panel. Then the building burns."

"Do you mean to tell me that I'm standing here in the wee hours of the morning so you can explain the mysteries of electrical codes and how to recognize accidental fires?" Tru asked acidly.

"No. No, not at all. Don't you get it? We've had two such fires. Remember? Some guy was running out of this basement and away from this fire. The fires started exactly the same way."

"You said that happens."

"Not exactly the same way. Not each time. See, here there is deep rolling charring and broad heat damage in and around the area of the service panel. The typical V pattern is particularly visible above the panel on this huge wooden beam the panel's mounted on," C. B. said, throwing the beam of light in various directions as she talked.

"If you say so," Tru said at the dizzy dancing light.

"Yeah, I do."

"From everything you've said, it still sounds like an accidental fire. Service panels exploding. What's your point? The guy could have been a derelict sneaking a sleep in an abandoned building and damn lucky he didn't get burned up too," Tru reasoned.

"Could have been, but the explosion, the eyewitness's statement about orange flames, and the thick black smoke that the first responders saw say something completely different," C. B. asserted.

"Meaning what?"

"Meaning, my dear detective, that orange flames generally have a particular temperature, somewhere around 1700 to 1800 degrees, too hot for an initial electrical fire. And black smoke combined with that flame color, even if the caller wasn't a good arbitrator of hues or casts, indicates the use of an accelerant. I'm betting on gasoline or kerosene," C. B. announced with a hint of triumph in her voice.

"Are there any signs of cans or other containers the perpetrator might have brought with him?" Tru asked as C. B.'s analysis increased her earlier speculations that Darrell Mawson's death might have been a well-staged murder.

"No. That's not necessarily what he may have used. I've got to get some crime scene protection in here, get a dog and come back when it is light. Then we can look for the missing pieces to this little puzzle."

"I can get some officers to protect this site. They're going to hate doing doughnut duty."

"Doughnut duty?"

"Yeah. Sitting on your rump and waiting for someone else to come along, do the work, and get the glory. Not that there is ever much glory. Doughnut duty's a good assignment if you don't like action or your worse nightmare if you're a rookie. I hated it when I was in patrol."

"I can believe that."

"What in the world do you want a dog for? You don't think you're going to be able to track an arsonist through the streets of Kansas City. Surely you don't think this retired cattle town is still a part of the old west, do you?" Tru asked, wondering if C. B. had lost her mind.

"Not hardly," C. B. said chuckling.

"Well, then?"

"An arson dog. I need a dog trained to sniff out accelerant like gasoline, turpentine, and such. The fire department in Saint Joseph has one. I'm going to ask to borrow it and its trainer. It's a special breed and a special skill. The dog will be able to locate any debris that has the slightest hint of accelerant on it," C. B. explained.

"No kidding. I don't remember ever hearing about a dog that can do that. Bomb sniffing dogs, yes. Drug sniffing dogs, sure. But a dog that sniffs out fire accelerants? Never," Tru said, shaking her head in amazement.

"They've been in use for some time. You've probably never had the opportunity to see one in action. There aren't too many of them, but in this case I'm going to use what I can borrow. The circumstances make it feel right."

"I agree. If your experience and the situation you've explained surrounding the fire are correct,

we'd be remiss if we didn't check it out," she said as
C. B. stood closer to her. Tru felt an arm slide
around her waist.

"Well," C. B. said as her hand laid lightly on
Tru's hip. "That's what I wanted to show you and
try to convince you of. The fires may be connected.
Same modus operandi, same techniques . . . maybe. I
need your backing to request the arson dog and your
authority to protect this scene with some of your
officers. Do we have a deal?" C. B.'s enthusiasm was
apparent in her voice.

C. B.'s touch welded Tru to the spot where she
stood. Tru's body shivered from the combination of
the cool, dank basement and the desire to respond in
kind to C. B.'s touch.

"You're freezing," C. B. said as she felt the shiver
run through Tru's body. "Come here," she invited
and opened her heavy firefighter's coat.

Before Tru could protest, before she could decide
that she should protest, C. B. gently pulled Tru
toward her and tucked her inside the coat. Tru
rested stiffly against the warmth that had been
offered.

"I've had just about enough of this," Tru said
with a menacing tone.

"You have, have you?"

"Yes, I have."

"I thought . . ." C. B. said, faltering.

"I've had enough of this to know I want more.
But I wonder if you know what kind of trouble
you're in," Tru said as she clasped the back of C. B.'s
neck and lowered her face to meet her lips.

Their lips teased, touched, and came together in

searching passion. Long moments slipped away in the embrace in the dark.

As Tru released her, C. B. parted her lips in anticipation. "No, I don't know what trouble I'm in. But I'm hoping it's just a little more than I deserve."

"Maybe a bit more," Tru said, drawing her in again.

"Come home with me?" C. B. asked, finding a hint of space not too far from Tru's earnest lips.

"Is it close?"

"River Quay close enough for you?"

"Let me call the road patrol first."

"Good point."

"First things first. We've got to get someone here to stand by while you get hold of the arson dog and I get a search warrant."

"We can wait on everything but the security of the crime scene until tomorrow, can't we?" C. B. asked, wondering if Tru was trying to evade her.

"Absolutely," Tru asserted and pulled C. B.'s lips back to her mouth again.

Back up at street level, the twenty minutes they had to wait for a patrol unit to arrive seemed like a week. After the officers arrived, C. B. opted to leave her arson investigation van where it was parked. She rode with Tru to the River Quay. It was a sensual, somewhat perilous drive as she tempted traffic and fate by warming her hands on the heat rising from Tru's blue jeans.

Chapter 10

C. B.'s loft apartment was located on the corner of Campbell and Fourth Streets. The front of the building had a massive clock nestled in the top tower of the four-story building. It was two-thirty in the morning, dark, with a rising southwesterly wind. C. B. guided Tru to the parking area beside the building and leaned over to kiss her again as she turned the car's engine off. C. B.'s hands found Tru's small breasts hiding under the leather jacket and massaged them with her large warm hands.

"If you keep that up, we'll never get inside," Tru said, freeing her mouth from C. B.'s. "And I definitely want to get inside."

"Come on, then," C. B. said, reaching across Tru to open the door.

They hurried up the sidewalk together. C. B. held her coat open for Tru and tried to protect her from the rising wind as they made a dash toward the security door. Once inside they walked to the old freight elevator and swung the gates open. The ride up to the fourth floor seemed interminable. They passed the time easily. Tru found herself awash with the immediacy of her desires and pressed C. B.'s back into the clapboard walls of the elevator cage. She let her hands roam C. B.'s back and move to her breasts. She let the tips of her fingers explore the soft material of C. B.'s turtleneck sweater and then moved them down to her firm stomach.

"Careful," C. B. warned. "If you keep that up, I'll take you here, and you'll never see whether I make my bed in the morning."

The elevator chimed out the approach of the fourth-floor landings, and Tru let her face rest on C. B.'s breasts. "Saved by the bell," she responded.

"Not yet." C. B. grabbed hold of the gliding elevator door and pushing it out of their way. "A few more feet."

Tru followed C. B. down the wide corridor and waited as patiently as she could while C. B. fumbled with the keys in her hand. The door opened, and they stepped inside to a softly lit great room. C. B. shut the door, reached behind Tru, and turned the lights up ever so slightly. A second flip of a switch sounded on the wall panel behind her, and Tru heard the soft refrains of k. d. lang's *Drag* album begin somewhere in the distance.

"That's a little overstated, isn't it?" Tru said, laughing up into C. B.'s face.

"Some might think so, but I like music and want it when I want it. I want it now," she said and turned to sweep Tru up into her arms.

"Are we still talking about music?"

"Only partly," C. B. said as she carried Tru across the room, past the high, wide windows, and toward the bedroom.

"You sure we're not rushing this?" Tru asked, wondering where that question came from.

"You've been inviting me since the other day. In particular, and if I remember right, you're the one who kissed me first," C. B. said as she put Tru on the bed. "Maybe I should be asking you what the flirting eyes and saucy mouth mean, if not an open invitation?"

"I wasn't the one in your face. I wasn't the one who was trying to control and hog the investigation. You were doing that," Tru protested.

"Who was it that couldn't, wouldn't, get my name right? Who was it that stared at me like I was standing in the nude in that burned-out wreck of a building? Weren't you around there somewhere?" C. B. replied as she helped Tru off with her coat.

"Might have been me. But you started it. You're the one who stuffed me into her coat."

"Like you hated it?"

"No, not like I hated it. And not like I know

what I'm doing here now, except that I want to be," Tru said and pulled C. B. down on the bed next to her.

C. B. leaned over and kissed Tru's forehead. "I'd like you to remember that you said that later. I'd like for you to want to be here in my arms later and not regretting what you did."

"You think I'll have something to regret?" Tru said as little fire alarms of her own jangled obnoxiously in her head. *Like Marki. If Marki ever finds out, will she forgive me? Can I forgive myself?*

"I see that crease running across your forehead even in this light," C. B. said in a worried tone. "We can stop now. This doesn't have to go any farther. I'd like it to, but it doesn't have to."

"I want you," Tru asserted. "I wanted you when you came trudging out of the shadows in that burned building. I don't want to have to analyze this. I don't want to rationalize or dissect this," Tru insisted.

"You're sure," C. B. asked again.

"Come here and see how sure I am."

Hands reached for hands and mouth yearned for mouth as they stretched across the bed. Tru reached up, gently ran her fingertips along C. B.'s strong jawline, and followed it to the dimple in her chin. Her thumb played across C. B.'s face until she cupped the fine chin in her hand. C. B. watched the play of emotions flutter across Tru's face and wondered what the eyes were reading, what they thought, and what they needed.

Tru raised her face to look into C. B.'s eyes as an unbidden grin slickered on her lips. Their lips came together in a velvety whispering touch. Tongues darted tentatively at each other and tasted the first slippery churning between them.

The vigorous mutual interest that had been sparked in the burned theater made them tentative now. Careful explorations, experimental maneuvers, and prudent assertions waltzed them toward their meeting. Careful touching waited for signaled acceptance as the tempo vaulted and swelled, pulling them along toward elevated harmonies.

Clothes disappeared, and their yearning began to seek its satisfaction in earnest.

There were no spoken questions, no analysis of act or demand assaulting Tru's ears. No questions, no prying, no searching for greater meaning than the thrill she sought in C. B.'s arms. The release, the instinct for an open door to escape rallied Tru to incendiary desire.

Hiding from yourself? A frequently asked question from Marki jabbed Tru's mind. *Quiet,* Tru ordered the noxious prying. *I don't want to think. I want to feel, to be, and to touch. I simply want to be.* Tru shut out the questioning voice.

C. B.'s long naked body covered Tru with its warmth. Tru quivered under the touch, weight, and silken sweep that covered her. Her response was immediate. All prudent, haunting reflections vanished as her arm muscles flexed and lifted C. B. with the intent to devour her.

Tru gave C. B. little opportunity to think as she sought the center of her being with her fingers and mouth. She let her fingers slide over C. B.'s hips and down her legs. Around the tender flesh of C. B.'s left

114

knee Tru felt the telltale signs of healed wounds and creased flesh.

"An old battle scar," C. B. said quietly as she felt Tru's fingers hesitate on the scars.

"Does it bother you to have me touch them?"

"No . . . the fire took away a lot of the nerve endings from there, and the operations took a lot more. Does it bother you?"

"No. I'm only sorry that you were so hurt," Tru said as she solicitously kissed the marred knee before continuing her journey up to the place where she wanted to create a different, gentler blaze for C. B.

C. B. rose on her knees and opened herself. She rocked forward in incessant response against Tru's mouth. The movement pulled her tantalizingly free and then back again onto the finger she discovered penetrating her ass. There was no place to go that didn't send her mind into riot or make her want to scream. Lovingly tortured, held, and hungered for, she was trapped between heaven and nirvana.

Tru pushed harder and slowly increased the tempo as she felt C. B.'s vagina stretch toward her, urging her to do the best her cultivated tonguing could. Tru played her and strummed her like the juice harp she'd become. Then Tru asked more from her, bewildering her as she tickled and plucked at a swaying nipple with her free hand. C. B. confronted her need, reacted to Tru's slippery request. And in her response unintentionally asked for more until she thought she could no longer stand another precious second of the molten charge between her legs.

From the depths of C. B. a whirlwind shuddered to life, lifting her, tossing her aloft on its turbulent upheaval. Her hands clasped Tru's hands, and she rose, arching back, holding on against the searing consummation.

Tru increased her efforts, holding, drinking in each shiver and resonating palpitation that C. B. offered. She looked up and watched the bowing full form hovering above her and reveled in the rapture she'd called to C. B.'s face.

C. B.'s arching back, shuddering arms, and legs weakened in their exertion. She whimpered throatily and collapsed slowly against the length of Tru's body. Tru let her tongue glide as C. B. passed, up from the sweet wetness, across the heaving belly to catch the first breast that swayed past her mouth. C. B. bent her head, her mouth agape, seeking the lips that touched the strained nerves of her flesh and whispered her name. Mouth sought mouth as hungry tongues wrestled for slippery dominance.

Tru wanted more. She had warned C. B. and was now determined to satisfy her need for the ardent response she wanted to drag from C. B. She would demand it, pull it from her slowly, and ignite her again. She wanted to see her quaver, shiver, laugh, and cry in synchrony. She wanted everything C. B. offered and everything C. B. might not know she had to give.

Tru moved slowly under C. B.'s body. She let her hands and fingertips smooth and stoke at C. B.'s skin till she felt quivering begin again beneath her touch. She raised her hips, pressing and lifting against C. B.'s thighs. There, there, and there. Firmly and absolutely, she rocked and swayed the pliable flesh above her until she heard honeyed gurgling pour from C. B.'s lips. Tru inched down, her mouth open, letting her lips and tongue suck and slide again on the sweet, heated sweat that she'd wrung from the woman over her.

Tru reached up, cupping her hands under C. B.'s armpits and raised her ever so slightly so as not to miss the opportunity to clasp her mouth on the belly-button pouting in its hollow. As Tru kissed the tight little nub, C. B. groaned and slipped slightly sideways. Tru easily caught her, let her slide, but kept her firmly in control. She didn't want C. B. to get away.

Tru could hear C. B.'s murmured voice as she lay next to her. She took it as a sign of encouragement and responded in kind. Tru's tongue flicked at the mound of dark hair, coursed between the ruby red, and teased along the inner edge of C. B.'s left leg. Tru's teeth gently nibbled the back of C. B.'s knee, letting her mouth wander upward again to gently nip at the sweet flesh.

Tru licked her lips in anticipation. She wanted the taste of C. B. on her way to orgasm, in the middle of orgasm, and the rarefied taste she anticipated after a searing thrust of orgasm. Tru wanted the vitality of her orgasm, the sharing of love's fleeting grand mal, completion, and everything that would come with it. Tru wanted to feel, touch, and envelop the body spasms she wanted C. B. to experience.

She moved forward, upward along the sleek firm flesh as her hands parted C. B.'s legs ever so slightly. She moved forward, licking her lips, the fine wiry hairs, the cloaking flesh of the clitoris as she began coaxing and beckoning it to fill her. A low, animal growl rumbled through C. B.'s chest as she pressed wantonly into Tru. With passion self-centered, wanting, and hiding nothing, she spilled forward and gave up to Tru's persistent demands.

She reeled, swayed, and shuddered. Tru returned the moan and suffered her own petit mal release. C. B.'s response charged Tru with inspiration. The night embraced the lovers until C. B. pleaded release and sweet mercy from her captor.

Tru kissed C. B.'s love-bruised lips, making them tremble and quiver toward her again. A giggle escaped Tru's mouth in pleasure. She reached up, let the palms of her hands slide along hips, across C. B.'s breasts, and up to where her ribs flared and fell rhythmically in fatigue. Pulling her to her, Tru kissed C. B.'s dry mouth, the corner of her closed eyes, and gently urged her to rest in her arms. C. B. lay down next to her, faced her, and held her as close as she could.

Tru's mind reeled. Small rivers of desire slipped through her body and made her shiver. Her mind's eye incautiously recounted the resplendent woman's body dancing to the tune her tongue had played.

"Are you cold? Is it chilly in here?" C. B. asked, feeling the tremble run the length of Tru's body.

"No. It's fine. Everything is fine."

"You're trembling. Is it because you think I might be remiss in my attentions to you?"

"You haven't been remiss in a thing. You're fine, wonderful."

"And you're satisfied to let it go at that? Let me do all the receiving and you do all the giving?" C. B. said as she raised herself up on her elbow to look intently at Tru.

"I'm great. Sharing has nothing to do with it.

118

This isn't a game of evens," Tru said, letting her hand find its way to the slight curve of C. B.'s hip.

"Maybe not. I hadn't expected you to be so over-powering. You surprised me."

"I surprised you?"

"With your vivacity. I feel weak as a kitten."

"Good. That was the plan," Tru confided.

"That was your plan. Aren't you even just the tiniest bit interested in my plans?" C. B. said, letting the palm of her hand slide down Tru's sweat-slicked back.

"Hmm," Tru breathed as her eyes fluttered shut at the sensation C. B.'s hand sent through her body. "A bit," she breathed.

C. B. raised herself on her elbow, touched Tru until she lay back, exposing herself, and trusting in her hunger. C. B. let her mouth visit Tru's small round breasts as her hand circled lower, ever nearer an ambitious intention. Her fingers stroked between the curling hairs and fleetingly brushed the engorged clitoral shaft. Feeling Tru's hips gyrate, she let the fingers linger on the threshold and then plunge deep inside. The wet walls gasped and grabbed at the fingers, opened and clutched again in invitation.

That was what C. B. wanted. She wanted to feel her own desire mirrored in Tru's response. She wanted to have it all, to feast on it, and take delight in Tru as she had felt delighted with Tru. Slowly, taking her time, the night danced toward day as C. B. unwittingly began to release Tru from the specters of her demons.

* * * * *

Friday the sun reached toward the sky and stole like a secret lover from its bed of rest. The morning glared through the crisp October haze and brightened the sky.

Tru rolled over and snuggled into the arms of the woman who held her. Her eyes opened, and she saw C. B.'s eyes smile tentatively at her. Tru reached up, stroked the straying salt-and-pepper hairs near C. B.'s left ear, and smiled in return.

"Good morning."

"Good morning yourself," Tru laughed.

"Do you suppose this means that the one thing that has changed is that we won't be fighting over the merits of arson cases or our respective investigative techniques?" C. B. ventured.

"It might not be the only thing that's changed," Tru confided absently.

"Meaning?" C. B. said, wondering at the insinuation in Tru's voice.

"Meaning," Tru said, changing the subject as she pulled C. B. into her waiting arms, "if you're not too sleepy, I intend to have breakfast in bed," she said as she let her right hand stray beneath the covers toward C. B.'s sensitive salt and peppered mound.

Chapter 11

"You're late," Bob Jones called to Tru from his office as she walked down the staggered expanse of cubicle offices in the homicide division. He had seen her when he glanced up from his paperwork. He watched the elevator doors open and close behind her. He felt himself rile slightly as she strolled into the area as if she didn't have a care in the world. At the sound of his voice, Tru looked in his direction, nodded, and walked toward his office.

"You're beginning to bark as loud as Captain Rhonn," Tru said, entering his office and closing the door behind her. She stood in front of his desk dressed in charcoal-gray slacks, gold silk shirt, and black double-breasted jacket. She watched his eyes and let a small grin dash across her face.

"That's because he's been chewing on my ass all morning. Where the hell have you been?"

"Don't ask and I won't tell," Tru responded, shifting her overcoat from her shoulder to one of the chairs in front of Jones's desk.

"That's not the answer I was looking for."

"I was busy."

"Too busy to call in, too busy to tell me why you didn't intend to be here at eight sharp? This better be good," Jones warned. "And the forensic pathologist, Dr. Camellia Houghin, has been calling for you since seven-thirty."

"It was . . . is good." Tru faltered as she tried to shift her mind away from the mental image of C. B. in her arms. "I was on a follow-up. There was another arson last night. You ought to know that from the call-out sheets. Anyway, the fire department's arson investigator thinks there might be a connection."

"OK. Stay on it, but don't play with it. And for godsake, find out what Dr. Houghin wants, will you? The good captain has assigned me to one of those make-nice public appearances. I can't waste my time trying to keep track of you for him." Jones huffed and shifted his large bulk in the chair.

"I'll try to keep you out of trouble," Tru promised.

"It's not me I'm worried about. You're one of his

least favorite people, and I seem to spend a lot of my precious time trying to keep him from having you for lunch. That reminds me, I had a very irate Ronald Rinhart call and want to know how to file a complaint against you."

"Rinhart? Oh, that guy. He owns the Genesse. I can imagine what his problem is. He's an obnoxious victim. Told me he knew very important people, wanted back in the building before I'd let him. It's nothing. On the other hand, the captain . . . is irate because he hasn't figured out how to make this an all-male squad. He's a chauvinist, and you know it. He's also mad because I know how to do my job and mostly I'm good at it."

"Doesn't take the whip from his hand."

"No, it doesn't, but I'm counting on you to be right and fair about things. He's still smarting from that routing he took from the administration over his last little attempt to do me in."

"Served him right too. Just don't help him. Play smart, OK? Rinhart said he's coming down to the public relations bureau to file a complaint. If I were you, I'd make sure my ducks were in a row. Otherwise, it will give the captain something to harangue you about."

"As smart as I can," Tru said, retrieving her coat from his chair and leaving his office.

At her desk she made a number of quick notes after logging on to her computer. There was so much to do, and time seemed to be slipping through her fingers. Two fires in two nights. She wondered at the frequency of the fires and worried that two might not be the end. She picked up the phone, dialed the coroner's office, and waited while the answering receptionist routed her call.

"Dr. Houghin," the voice on the other end responded.

"Camellia, this is Tru. I hear you've been looking for me?"

"Tru, girl, you're damn right. We've got bodies stacked up back to the loading dock. Damn bunch of gang-related shootings and stabbings the last four days. What's the world coming to?"

"I was hoping you were calling about the arson victim," Tru said, wondering if everyone was having a bad Friday but her.

"I was. Can you be here by eleven? I've got Mawson scheduled for that time. I'm going to do him myself and let my underlings deal with the gang victims. I'd take a toasty any day over senselessness."

"Will you be in a better mood by the time I get there?"

"Maybe. It will be nice to see you again. However, it's a shame we only see each other while peering into dead bodies."

"I know, Camellia. It's not like when I was in training in your office. We should, however, make a commitment to get together and have supper somewhere downtown," Tru suggested.

"That would be nice. Of course, you know we'd simply wind up talking shop."

"That wouldn't take away from the pleasure of your company," Tru responded. "Do you want to try for next Wednesday?"

"I'll mark it on my calendar. We'll decide later where and exactly when."

"Deal. Oh, by the way, I'm going to bring an arson investigator with me for the autopsy. Is that all right?"

"As long as he doesn't get in my way or cause a commotion. How many burned bodies has he observed in autopsy?"

"She, it's a she, and I don't know. I didn't ask," Tru confided, wondering what C. B.'s response would be to the grisly event.

"You know how I am. If she can't stand the heat, I don't want her in my kitchen."

"Right, Camellia. She's been on the job for some time. I'm sure she's been acclimated. And I'll warn her about you," Tru said, chuckling. Tru heard voices in the background in Camellia's office.

"Got to go. See you at eleven."

Shaking her head, Tru lowered the already dead receiver.

Dr. Camellia Houghin hadn't changed, and at fifty-five, apparently wasn't ever going to. There apparently wasn't any need. Tru had met the good doctor several years ago when she'd been assigned to the coroner's office for training in medico-legal death investigation. It had been an opportunity few detectives ever experienced. Dr. Houghin had put Tru through her paces, required absolute attention, learning effort, and instructional diligence. Tru had given herself over to the educational experience and tutelage for six long months. All the effort had paid off when Tru had been promoted to detective sergeant, even over the protests of Captain Rhonn, two months ago. Tru thought that if nothing else she should take her mentor and friend to dinner and spend some of the promotional raise on her.

As she turned back to her computer to mark her daily calendar with the scheduled autopsy, her desk phone rang.

"North," she said as she punched the speakerphone button.

"That's not a very nice tone, sweetness." Marki's voice broadcast through Tru's small office cubicle and bounced beyond its stunted walls.

"Crap," Tru breathed and quickly grabbed the receiver.

"That's even worse." Marki's voice sounded in her ear.

"I'm sorry, Marki. I had the phone on speaker. I don't think I want everyone in this reverberating dungeon to hear you call me sweetness."

"Apology accepted, I think. But besides that, where have you been? I've been calling your apartment for days. Didn't you get my message?"

"Ah . . ."

"I didn't think so. I hear the department's been keeping you awfully busy in my absence?"

"Yes," Tru said.

"What sort of mischief have you been up to?"

Tru swallowed guilt. "We've had a homicide by arson. At least that's what it looks like. I'm still working on that child-abuse case and finishing up on the murder-suicide I had before you left. How's your stepfather?"

"Better. It was my mother that I was actually worried about. She loves the lout, and even with fifty thousand tubes stuck in him in intensive observation, he can still manage to talk her into a worried frenzy," Marki's voice seethed.

"That's a pity. Was it his heart again?"

"It is, but the old fart keeps up his ranting verbal abuse sucking on oxygen without missing a beat. I swear if I hadn't come here, she'd be standing by his bedside every minute listening to his tirades. As it is, I can deflect a little of it and make sure she gets her rest too."

"You sound tired. Are you getting your rest?" Tru asked in real concern.

"Some. Fortunately, the ICU only allows one ten-minute visit every three hours. It's supposed to be for the patients. But from what I've seen here watching other people in the waiting rooms, I think it's the only way for a family to keep from becoming the next ailing batch while they stand vigilance with loved ones."

"I wish I could help somehow," Tru said consolingly.

"It's all right. Knowing that you're there is what counts. I'll be home as soon as I can. I want to see you, be with you, and hold you again. I need my strength back, and making love to you would be the best way I can think of," Marki said, lowering her voice affectionately.

"Yes, I, ah . . ." Tru faltered.

"Got to go. My mother is waving to me. I hope she wants to go to the hospital cafeteria to get some coffee. Anyway, I'm not going to come home until he's out of intensive care. This is going to take a little longer than I thought. I'll call you this weekend. Try to stay out of trouble."

"You bet," Tru said, finding it difficult to swallow.

"Love you."

"Love you, too."

Tru sat staring blankly at the phone after Marki

hung up. A world of mixed emotions roared through her. She felt deep affection for Marki, but Marki had begun pushing and pulling at her in ways that made her uncomfortable. Then there was C. B. The new, exciting, and enthralling C. B. Tru's mind raced between one and the other, and there was no safety or certainty in sight. She was grateful for the reprieve. Marki wasn't coming back until sometime later in the week, and Tru knew she needed that time and more.

"A fine mess," Tru mumbled to herself as she left her desk and walked toward the elevators.

As she passed the receptionist station near the elevators, Tru turned to the woman to speak. The receptionist looked up from the receiver and waved a halting hand at Tru. Tru waited for the woman to get finished with her call.

"Yes, detective?"

"Would you call this number for me and ask Inspector Belpre to be at the coroner's office at eleven? Tell her Dr. Houghin always starts when she says she's going to start. It wouldn't do to be late."

"Of course," the woman said, taking the card Tru offered. "Do you want to talk to her?"

"Not right now," Tru said as she got into the elevator. "Tell her I need to do some think—that is, I need to do some *check*ing on some things. I'll meet her there," she said as the doors slid closed. *Hell of a mess,* her mind repeated as the elevator jerked to life under her feet.

* * * * *

Niangua Heights, Missouri, Marshal Bill Vernon sat in his new-to-the-department used highway patrol car and admired the vehicle's highly polished finish. The town council had purchased the new patrol car last month after a long, drawn-out fiscal battle. But he had won. With fewer than fifty thousand miles on it, the retired highway patrol car would be a long sight better than the wheezing Fairlane he'd been driving. He patted his radar unit fondly.

"Speeders beware," he said, daring the potential contributors to the town's coffers to try to outrun him now. He sat behind a large outdoor billboard and patiently waited for an unsuspecting tourist. He knew someone would be along. It was October. City slickers from Kansas City and Saint Louis could be counted on to breeze through his town on vacation and gape at the fall blaze spreading through the leaves of the trees. The rarefied oak, elm, and maple forests surrounding the Lake of the Ozarks could catch the breath of the most jaded observer. Marshal Vernon knew that the motorists' eyes would be on the trees and not on the road. He didn't have to wait long.

The new blue Taurus easily banked the long curve south of where Marshal Vernon sat patiently waiting. The marshal trained his radar unit on the approaching vehicle and initially clocked the car doing 65 miles per hour as it hit the straightaway.

"That's ten over," Marshal Vernon breathed, but he kept his finger from pulling the lock-on trigger in anticipation of the motorist accelerating on the flat.

He wasn't disappointed. The car seemed to hunker

down to the road and charge along the leaf-torn stretch.

"Seventy-five. Gotcha," Marshal Vernon said, locking the vehicle's speed into the radar gun. He shifted his car from PARK to DRIVE and pulled out from behind the sign with his overhead emergency lights flashing.

He could tell when the driver saw him, and he chuckled to himself as the nose of the car almost scraped the roadbed as the driver rapidly applied the brakes.

"Don't hurt yourself," the marshal whispered to himself in caution to the driver. "Just pull over to the side, and we'll do fine."

The car stopped twenty feet to the south of where the marshal had pulled out his patrol car. The driver rolled down his window as if to question the reason for the stop. Marshal Vernon put his left arm outside his car window and motioned for the driver to pull his vehicle up and in front of where he sat. The car pulled slowly forward past the patrol car and came to a stop.

Emergency lights still flashing, Marshal Vernon pulled in behind the blue car and parked. He saw the driver start to get out of the car and quickly grabbed the public address microphone from its stand.

"Stay in your car," the marshal ordered. "Stay in for your safety and mine. Be patient. I'll be up there in a minute." Marshal Vernon reached for the police radio microphone and called central dispatch.

"Dispatch, Niangua 230."

"Go ahead, 230," the dispatcher responded.

"Dispatch, would you run me a wants, warrants, and registration information on a Missouri BR00997?"

"Sure thing. Stand by."

Marshal Vernon flipped open his citation book and began filling in the court date and vehicle description particulars while he waited for the information he'd requested from dispatch. The twenty miles an hour over the posted speed limit on his little stretch of the highway would cost the driver more than eighty-five dollars in fine and court cost combined. He hoped the mayor would appreciate his efforts to pay for the new patrol car.

"Vernon, do you have the driver with you?" the dispatcher's voice said cautiously over the radio.

"No, what's up, Betsy?"

"We got a hit on that car. It refers to an APB. Stand by while I run it up."

"All right," Marshal Vernon said, assuring the dispatcher as he reached down and unsnapped the catch on his Glock .44. A hit could mean anything from an expired registration to a bank robber. He wasn't going to take any chances. He tossed the traffic ticket book on the car seat and intently watched the interior of the car in front of him for any strange movements.

"Vernon," the radio crackled his name.

"Yeah, Betsy. Go ahead."

"Vernon, I'm sending you some backup. Charlie Edmond with the county is about two miles away."

"What's up, Betsy?" Marshal Vernon said, feeling the hairs on the back of his neck stand on end.

"The APB says the car is reported as stolen." The

dispatcher's voice had drawn taut. "The driver is a murderer, Vernon. You stay put and keep yourself out of harm's way. Edmond is coming as fast as he can."

"Not to worry, Betsy," Marshal Vernon said as he drew his Glock from its holster.

Thirty minutes later Marshal Vernon and Deputy Edmond had secured the protesting driver, cuffed him, and made arrangements for the Taurus to be towed to town. Vernon whistled softly to himself as he drove down the main street toward the waiting jail. It had taken more than a little gentle persuasion to get the driver into the secured backseat of the patrol car. Edmond had made the man "do the chicken" by twisting the cuffs up high and away from his back. The driver of the stolen car ranted and raved in the backseat.

It took enormous self-control for the marshal not to turn to the man and say something about the heap of trouble he was in.

Chapter 12

Tru North found forensic pathologist Camellia
Houghin in the second large morgue room of the
coroner's office. She was standing over the wet-suited
charred remains of fire victim Mawson. It was five
after eleven, and she'd begun the process of the
autopsy. As Tru walked the length of the cold,
brightly-lit room, Dr. Houghin looked up as the sound
of approaching feet echoed across the ceramic-tiled
floor.

"You're late," Dr. Houghin said as Tru stood
across the table from her.

"I know. My apologies. I got hung up in traffic. We're supposed to be joined by an arson investigator, but I imagine she's caught in the same maze of yellow-and-white striped traffic barrels I was," Tru offered.

"No matter. Mr. Mawson isn't going anywhere. The family came in yesterday wanting to help identify the body, for all that would have been worth. I explained to them that it would not be necessary. I didn't want his mother exposed to his condition. Not that she could have identified him. It would have simply traumatized her and I like to avoid that when I can. Anyway, I had Harry do the X rays earlier this morning. A complete set, head to toe. He'll have them for us later. Now, as you can see," Dr. Houghin said, pointing to the head of the victim, "he's also removed the upper and lower jaws for charting purposes."

"I don't remember doing any fire victims when I worked with you those six months," Tru said, trying not to fix her gaze on the vacant, ravaged remains of the face in front of her. She fixed her gaze at the top of the victim's cap and left it there.

"Maybe nothing this wrecked," Dr. Houghin commented. "We removed the jaws because we want to make charts to compare them to previous X rays we will obtain from the dentists that his family said he used."

"Why do all of that?"

"It's a simple assurance measure. Although the family bravely identified him, I have to make sure. There's not much left of his face that even a mother or lover could or would want to identify. Protocol. Simple protocol."

"You're saying we got lucky. What with him conveniently leaving his clothes piled on the floor and his wallet with a set of car keys in the pants pockets. Otherwise we might not have known who he was. The rubber of the wet suit seems to have melted and adhered to his face and body. It's still going to make your job a little trying to conduct, isn't it?" Tru asked.

"A bit. It became his first layer of skin. But that's why I wanted the complete X rays. With this material and its response to the heat, if the body suffered any trauma before death, well, it could be complicated to recognize and assess."

"Detective North?"

Tru turned around and saw C. B. standing by the door at the far end of the room. She flashed a quick smile at C. B. and motioned for her to come to the examination table where she and Dr. Houghin stood.

C. B. slowly walked the length of the room, eyeing the drain tables where several more bodies lay waiting under wraps for their final exploration. Her eyes darted along the decks of closed stainless-steel shelving units, the rows of bright fluorescent lights, and the cool white walls.

"Glad you could make it," Tru said as C. B. stopped to stand a little behind her.

"Happy to be here," C. B. whispered.

"Really?" Tru said and looked at C. B.

"Well, not exactly happy to be here, but it's good to see you again."

"Ahem," Dr. Houghin interjected.

"Dr. Camellia Houghin, I'd like you to meet C. B. Belpre of the Arson Investigation Unit," Tru offered. And to C. B., "Dr. Houghin is the chief forensic pathologist for the city. Her name is legend."

"Nice to meet you," C. B. said.

"Same. So, what say we get to it?" Dr. Houghin said as she pulled the recording microphone down from its swing arm and clicked it on. "Dr. Camellia Houghin, chief forensic pathologist for the city of Kansas City, Missouri. The time is eleven-twenty. Observing investigators to the autopsy of tentatively identified victim are . . ." she said, continuing her opening remarks.

Two hours later, Tru and C. B. walked out of the building that housed the coroner's office and into a light October rain. The initial phases of the autopsy had been completed, leaving them with more questions than answers.

"Houghin will make sure I have a copy of the autopsy report and findings by Monday. Toxicology, dental, and the rest of the analysis results will be included. I hope we get a better picture of what's going on by then. In the meantime, I've got the search warrants ready whenever we need them for the arson sniffing dog," Tru said as she walked toward her car. "Do you want to go get some late lunch?"

"Does lunch come with conversation?"

"Sure. What would you like to talk about?" Tru said, cautiously.

"A little this and a little that."

"That could be arranged. Come on," Tru said, opening the door to her car.

Tru drove toward the plaza and a favorite lunch spot. Lorenzaki's was located on the edge of the plaza on Main. It had been a fixture in the area for twenty years. Tru had discovered it shortly after her assignment to the detective bureau. Lorenzaki, a small portly native of Crete, had transplanted himself and his aging mother to Kansas City, after he had received a scholarship for doctoral study in economics in the United States. He hadn't intended to be a restaurant owner. But when his mother became seriously ill, Lorenzaki left his studies, got a green card, and set up a small one-man restaurant featuring hearty European cuisine.

The meals were inexpensive and delicious. Then there was the entertainment of the place. The music over the radio was classical, the tables and chairs an odd assortment of sturdy card tables and liberated kitchen furniture, the decorations festooning the ceiling were posters of European vacations and plastic sausages, cheeses, and flags.

Then there was Lorenzaki himself, with haircut like one of the aging Beatles, wide open welcoming arms, a constant smile, and a memory like a steel trap. He would remember how much spice you liked, whether you cleaned your plate the last time you were in, and whether or not you had ever confided to him about anything. If you didn't want it remembered, you didn't tell it to Lorenzaki.

Tru and C. B. entered the shop and were immediately grabbed up and escorted to the first available card table.

"So long, you've not been here," Lorenzaki admonished Tru.

"I know, and my apologies. But I'm back, and I've brought a friend."

"Yo, I see. And how do you know our Tru?" Lorenzaki quizzed happily at C. B.

"We're working together on a case," C. B. responded. She sat in the chair Lorenzaki offered.

"Ah. So you are not an intimate of Tru's?" he said.

Tru and C. B. exchanged startled glances. Tru chuckled and raised a pleading hand to C. B.

"Lorenzaki and I have known each other for a long time. However, in the European vernacular, an *intimate* is a very good, long-time friend. Isn't that right, Loren?" Tru hastened to explain.

"Sure, sure, sure," he said, patting Tru's arm while he winked over her head at C. B. "Now what can I get for you ladies? Because today we have ..." He described the four courses of healthy, bone-warming dishes available and explained about the soup and sandwiches for the lighter appetites.

They ordered, and Lorenzaki hurried off to get their food. C. B. sipped the coffee he'd brought to their table and looked up at Tru expectantly.

"European vernacular?" she repeated at Tru.

"Of course it is," Tru asserted.

"I see. Then am I an intimate or not, in American vernacular?"

"After last night? How much more intimate do you think we can be?"

"A bit, quite a bit. Would you like to find out what and how?" C. B. offered lasciviously.

Tru looked around to see how close the other

diners were sitting and leaned forward, closer to C. B. "I would," she breathed and felt the tendrils of a blush threaten to rise to her face.

"Wonderful. First, though, we ought to have lunch, figure out what to do with the investigation, and see if we can find a way to catch our fire starter," C. B. suggested.

"We seem to be running a no-hitter," Tru remarked.

"It's early. Do you have a patience problem?"

"No," Tru said defensively and looked up to find C. B. smiling at her. "Well, sometimes, maybe a bit. Not where or when it counts, however. Speaking of patience, where's that fire-sniffing dog you were getting?"

"Honor Twin is on her way. Her trainer, Linda Sorenson, will meet us at the Genesse building at four. If I'm right about what I think is going on, it won't take too long and we can check out the theater, too," she said as Lorenzaki brought their lunch plates and set them before them.

"Honor Twin? Is that the dog's name?" Tru asked.

"Yes. Linda's a fan of mythology and a real dog lover. Her first arson dog, Checkers, died when some sleazeball she was having prosecuted a few years ago poisoned the animal. She was heartbroken. Honor Twin came from another litter by the same dam and sire. So, the name Honor Twin."

"Where do these dogs come from?" Tru said as she lifted another helping of Hungarian chicken to her mouth.

"They can come from anywhere. Linda prefers golden retrievers for their temperament and

139

sturdiness. It's the training that counts. Linda and both of her dogs trained in Connecticut. There's a specialized school there. The best in the country. The program lasts for five weeks. It really puts the potential arson dog and the master through the paces, from what she tells me.

"There's no tolerance for error. At the end of the training session, the dog is to successfully walk through a series of twenty scenes and identify each and every area where an accelerant may have been used. One hundred percent is required or the dog is rejected."

"No errors, no faults, no slack?"

"None. Neither dog nor handler can afford a miss or false-positive identification. Wouldn't look good in court. Once they're done, they return to the home fire department or fire marshal agency and practice every day of the dog's useful life. This goulash is great. Can you cook?" C. B. asked.

"Not so you would notice. I read *Bon Appétit*, as silly as that may seem. I just don't seem to be able to pull any of it off, however. I like good food, but I'm not very domestic. It's not the only way my mother believed she failed to properly socialize me. She might have been right," Tru heard herself confiding.

"No matter. I can cook up a storm. I found out a long time ago that if you like to eat, you have to learn how to cook. Or hire someone who can."

"You were saying the dog practices every day? Does that mean they go to fires every day? That's a tough assignment even in Kansas City or St. Joseph, isn't it?"

"No. They don't have to go to fire scenes unless

called. There are lots of jurisdictions that borrow Linda and Honor Twin. But when they're not at a scene, Linda puts Honor Twin through her paces at her home. She's got a practice wheel set up."

"A wheel?"

"Yeah, a big plywood wheel she rigged to a motor. It has different types of burned accelerant on it. She changes them every day. The order and types, that is. She does that so the dog doesn't get into any habits. Spins it and lets the dog loose to point out the areas of accelerant."

"Every day?"

"Every day, twenty tests a day, twice a day from what she tells me."

"Goddess, that's a lot of work."

"Well, Honor Twin is a tool. Like your gun. If you don't keep up the practice, you won't be as good at it and maybe at the worst possible moment. Besides, the training for the handler and dog usually runs a department somewhere between eight and ten thousand dollars. So they have to stay sharp."

"You said you thought it was arson. What else are you trying to find?"

"How he did it. What he used. And what he was doing when he got careless last time. I have a few hunches, but as you know, I can't take them to court. I have to find out exactly where the accelerant was used. Once I do that, then maybe I can see what we missed before."

"What do you mean? What *we* missed?" Tru said, raising a questioning eyebrow at C. B.

"Now come on. If there is an arsonist, he used an accelerant. It had to be delivered, made available to start the fire, and delayed long enough for him to get

141

away. Of course, last time he screwed something up and was seen. I'm betting that if Honor Twin can show me the source area, then we'll have the laboratory technicians examine the debris and source materials for the type of accelerant. Then . . ." C. B. said, spreading her arms.

"Then we'll know that much more about the bastard and get closer to identifying him," Tru finished C. B.'s thought for her.

C. B. let her fork rest on the edge of her plate and moved her chair back from the table.

"That was great. I'm so stuffed I don't know if I'll ever move again."

"That's a shame," Tru said, sipping her coffee.

"Oh?"

"I just mean that according to my watch we've got two whole hours before we have to meet Linda and Honor Twin. My place is a few blocks away. I suppose we could take a nap and let the meal digest. It's up to you?"

"A nap. Having a nap with you would be great. But we don't have to sleep the whole time do we?" C. B. said as she let her hand brush across Tru's fingertips.

"I thought you said you couldn't move." Tru laughed.

"Why don't we just see about that?" C. B. said as she tossed her money on the table, stood up, and held her hand out for Tru.

As Tru held the door to her second-floor apartment open for C. B., she felt a pang of guilt knowing that Marki wouldn't be back in town until later the next week. *There's been no commitment,* a small voice assured her in the back of her mind. *And there sure won't be if Marki finds out,* the voice returned.

"Well, what do you think," Tru said as she ushered C. B. into her living space.

"Fairly comfortable. I noticed you don't go in much for knickknacks," C. B. said as she looked from the sparsely furnished dining area, across the computer workstation, and into the living room.

"I don't like to spend time dusting it, and that's all those types of things are ever good for. Remember, I told you I wasn't very domestic."

"I seem to recall that. Does your lover clean for you?" C. B. said, walking toward the French doors of the veranda.

"My . . . lover?" Tru said with slow deliberation as her eyes darted about the rooms trying to find the telltale signs of Marki that she thought C. B. might have detected. She couldn't find a clue as to what C. B. might have seen or noticed.

C. B. turned to meet Tru's widened eyes as a slow smile crept across her face. "You know under inquiry, for a detective, you kinda break down like a cheap shotgun. You don't lie very well, that is, if that's what you were thinking about doing."

"I don't lie. However, I suppose there are times that I'm not completely revealing," Tru admitted defensively.

"It's all right," C. B. said, walking back to where Tru stood and putting a hand on Tru's arm. "It was a guess. I couldn't help from asking. How do you feel about it?"

"A guess? You just tossed out a guess?"

"Of course. It was a good guess, too. I figured it was a reasonable question to ask. You're an attractive woman. I simply figured that most women who love women would be attracted to a smart, professional, attractive woman such as yourself. Simple logic and burning curiosity on my part."

"You'd make a good investigator," Tru said, leading C. B. to the couch to sit down.

"Really? You think so? I have another question, but you don't have to answer it if you don't want to," C. B. said, taking Tru's hands into her own.

"Might as well ask."

"Here goes. Think of it as an interrogatory, like when attorneys are working on discovering how much people know and how much they're willing to say. There are several parts."

"Don't you think it's a little early in the day for twenty questions?" Tru said, trying to divert C. B. from the path she was taking.

"No. It's a perfect time. We have one night between us, and a lot of what feels like mutual desire. It doesn't matter where I stand, except I like firm footing. I don't care for surprises, so I have to ask a few questions. You don't have to say a thing. Silence would be an answer too. But whatever you do say will help me know where it is I want to stand and where I want to and can go. Deal?"

"Sort of. Hell, go ahead. Ask away," Tru said, trying to shrug nonchalantly as she reached for a cigarette.

C. B. looked at the glowing tip of the cigarette with envy but refrained from breaking her abstinence from that habit. "How long have you been in the relationship?"

"We've been dating for six months."

"Dating? It's interesting that you refrained from using the word *relationship*. Are you telling me there's no commitment to the dating? Are you unhappy with her? Is that why we were together last night? Or am I part of some open dating agreement you have with each other?"

"That's four questions."

"They are related. I said you didn't have to answer any question," C. B. said, regarding Tru through the rising smoke of the cigarette.

"Crap," Tru breathed heavily. Why were women always trying to quiz each other to death? If it wasn't Marki, it was someone else prying around inside her mind.

"OK. All right," Tru said in frustration. "Thing is, she's been pressuring me lately. Wanting me to commit, move in with her, and share her house. I need that like I need a hole in my head. I, I got out of that sort of sharing circumstance about ten months ago. I don't want to go back into a situation where I'm part of someone's collection of property, like another piece of furniture. I want something of my own, and I think I want to have balance in the sharing. An 'ours' thing rather than a predicament where it's all her stuff and me as an add-on."

"You got put out in the cold in that other relationship?"

"Well, it was February. Yeah, it was pretty damn cold, but that says more about the woman's heart than the weather," Tru conceded.

"So you're worried about being a kept woman? Or feeling like you're being kept with nothing to show for it if it all goes to rot?" C. B. said, leaning forward to brush loose strands of hair away from Tru's brow. Her fingers brushed Tru's cheeks and swept back along her shoulders and up to the base of her head. She felt the tension in the muscles of Tru's neck and began to massage them tenderly.

"I've been trying to figure out how to talk to her about it. Problem is, I don't get around to it. When I screw my courage up to try to mention something, she's prying into my life, asking questions about my past, and still insisting that we move in together," Tru commented. The frustration reflected itself on her face.

"You have a problem with people asking questions about you or your life," C. B. said as she shifted Tru to lean back into her arms. She rested against the back of the couch and held Tru.

"Not really," Tru said, feeling some of her tension easing as she nestled in the warmth C. B. offered. "For me, it's been difficult to . . . Things take time. I don't like to be rushed."

"Unless you're the one doing the rushing?" C. B. said quietly and kissed the back of Tru's neck.

Tru laughed at the revelation. "Yeah. That's fair. You're right, you know. I don't like to be rushed unless I'm the one doing the pushing."

"Otherwise it feels out of control," C. B. offered as she nibbled on Tru's left ear.

"Maybe."

"What's her name?"

"Who?"

"The other woman. No, maybe I'm the other

woman. What is the name of the woman who's trying to push you in a direction you're not ready to go?" C. B. said, knowing she could be tempting fate.

"Marki. Marki Campbell. She's a psychologist at the university. She's a good woman, really," Tru explained.

"I'm sure she is," C. B. agreed. The woman's name was Marki. C. B. knew that the strength of the competition, if there was to be one, would be dependent on the determination of that woman and Tru's hidden heart. She would have to meet Marki somehow. *Can't engage what you can't understand,* C. B. thought determinedly.

"I'm tired, aren't you? We didn't get much sleep last night," Tru said, swiftly changing the subject.

"Yes, I am. Why don't you lie down here beside me, and we'll take that nap you promised," C. B. suggested.

"Good," Tru said, as she and C. B. slid down onto the sofa and nestled in for the rest.

As she drifted off to sleep, C. B. had to quiet inner voices as they fought for her attention between ideas of contest with Marki, cautionary tales about interfering with lovers, and her own desire to have someone to have and hold again.

Tru shifted in her sleep in dreams warning of fire as a weapon and buildings blazing out of control.

Chapter 13

"That's Linda," C. B. said, waving to the woman standing by a burgundy van. Tru pulled up next to the curb at the Genesse Exchange building. "She's a pretty thing, isn't she," C. B. said more than asked.

Tru looked at the petite woman with long, dark-brown hair as she walked to the back of the van. She was pretty. The woman wore a tight-fitting utility jumpsuit of dark amber that was cinched at the waist by a wide black belt. An open, expressive face with a wide grin complemented the modest, full-bodied figure. As Linda opened the van doors, Tru watched a flash of long fingernails covered in dried-blood polish grab the leash on the golden-coated golden retriever.

"Straight as an arrow and a little homophobic too, I might add," C. B. told Tru in a whispered warning tone.

"The voice of experience?" Tru asked.

"Not hardly. Just a word to the wise. She's unwittingly a bit of a flirt, but I've watched her, and she does that with everyone. You know, some straight women don't seem to be able to turn it off. They get set in one mode of association being heavily male-dependent and it simply lapses over into every other human contact they make."

"That could be dangerous for her. Not to mention for some other poor schmuck."

"Without telling tales out of school, let's say that it has been. Makes her vulnerable to getting approached a lot by some folks with specific intentions. Male and female. I've seen some of the cruising. Never joined it though. My radar is more discerning than that."

"Good. Mixed signals can be dangerous."

"It's really not a matter of mixed signals. At least that's my take on it. The signals are there. Always. Nancy just hasn't figured out yet that she never stops broadcasting her seductiveness and allure to anyone in the vicinity. It's like she's handicapped and doesn't know it."

"Let's get to it, and I'm sure I can restrain myself," Tru said laughingly to C. B. "The straight or passingly curious have always been on my taboo list."

"A useful survival mechanism," C. B. agreed as she got out of the car.

149

"Nancy, good to see you again. I appreciate your taking the time to come and help us," C. B. said as she walked over to the van.

"No problem. Glad to do it," Linda Sorensen said as she shook the hand C. B. offered.

"I'd like you to meet a friend of mine. This is Detective Sergeant Tru North. She's conducting the homicide investigation in the fire."

"Nice to meet you. And who do we have here?" Tru said as she knelt down to pet the dog. The dog sat down.

"That's Honor Twin," Nancy said affectionately. "She's my best buddy. You smoke, don't you?"

"Yes, I do. Don't tell me my breath is bad?" Tru asked in surprise.

"No, I can't smell your breath, but Honor Twin sat down as you touched her. That tells me you've probably got a cigarette lighter on you and that you've recently used it to light up."

"Sitting down is the signal. I thought dogs like this, like drug and bomb dogs, usually dig or scratch around at the site where they detect something," Tru said. She stood up and looked at the dog in increasing interest.

"That's not the way Honor Twin's been trained. Scratching or rooting around an area where an accelerant was used could destroy or confuse the possibility of collecting the evidence. Honor Twin was trained to locate the source and announce it by sitting down. She'll stay at the spot until I release her by feeding her."

"A nice little reward system."

"Not just rewards. She only gets fed when she locates accelerant," Linda said, vigorously patting the dog and giving her a small handful of nibbles. "Isn't that right, girl?"

"She doesn't eat on a regular basis?"

"Sure she does. That's why we practice. She eats when she does the right thing in pretend, and we do that a lot. Trust me. She doesn't starve for food or affection," Linda said, patting the dog's full frame.

"Interesting. Where do you want to start?"

"The top. I like to go from the area where there's been the least amount of burning to the most. It will give me perspective and a chance for Honor Twin to do her best work. We'll be able to get a complete picture of where accelerants were used and maybe even a few places where they didn't have an opportunity to ignite. If we're lucky, there might be some accelerant in the surfaces of the structure to collect as evidence."

"I've got a camcorder I want to use, and C. B. has a backpack full of tools and glass evidence- collection jars. I'd like to come along and watch you work. Is that OK or would it interfere with the dog?"

"No problem. Once on the job, Honor Twin has only two things on her mind, finding places where accelerant might be located and getting fed if and when she locates them."

By six in the evening, the team had worked their way from the sixth floor to the third floor. Honor Twin had gone without a nibble reward as she padded her way through every room on every floor.

Tru walked behind C. B., Linda, and Honor Twin as she filmed their progress. She was beginning to wonder if the situation was hopeless when Honor Twin sauntered over to the area under and around the third-floor electrical service panel and sat down.

"That's a gotcha," Linda said as she gave Honor Twin her handful of rewards. "There's something here."

"Shit. I checked that area," C. B. said in exasperation.

"You don't have Honor Twin's nose."

"Thank the goddess for that," C. B. said, patting the dog's long snout. She shifted her backpack off her shoulder and knelt down to begin sifting through the burned rubble again.

"We'll go ahead and check the other floors. Tru, do you want to stay here or follow us?" Linda asked.

"I'll go with you. I want to complete the taping of the dog checking the building. C. B., don't get too far ahead of us before I get back. I want to film the evidence collection."

"No problem. I'm going to remove some of this top debris. It would have fallen down over the fire and where the accelerant was located anyway. I'll be here when you get back. You'll mark off any other accelerant location, right?"

"You bet."

Tru, Linda, and Honor Twin returned to C. B.'s location a little later. The bottom two floors and the basement were thoroughly searched, but no other suspicious locations had been found.

Tru knew that the rest of the day's work was going to involve grunt work. Linda and Honor Twin left, promising to fax a complete report and their respective credentials to C. B. at the fire marshal's office.

Tru stayed with C. B. and with the slow task of debris removal. Layer after layer of debris was removed with pieces placed carefully in the glass jars. Night was closing in, and the room darkened except where Tru held the video camera light over the laboring C. B.

"Well, damn. Will you look at this," C. B. exclaimed as she removed the last layer of fire debris from under the electrical panel.

Tru leaned over C. B.'s shoulder, held the lights over the place C. B. pointed to, and tried to make out what C. B. was pointing at. Tru shook her head; she failed to understand what she was supposed to be looking at.

"What?"

"This, this damn thing, and there," C. B. insisted.

"All I see is what looks like a tiny piece of melted plastic and a rabbit turd."

"It just so happens that the bit of melted plastic and rabbit turd, as you call it, is the evidence. Not all of it. The remaining accelerant may be locked in some of these charred boards and the electrical panel itself."

"We take it all," Tru directed.

"You bet we take it all. And first thing tomorrow morning we go back to the theater, and I bet I get to collect more melted plastic and rabbit turds there. You up to it?"

"No rest for the weary," Tru conceded.

"That's *wicked*. The saying is, No rest for the *wicked*," C. B. corrected.

153

"Have it your way. I want to take this to the lab and have them run spectrographic analysis on it tonight. The longer we wait the colder the guy's tracks become."

"Agreed. But do you think you can find anyone to do the work tonight?"

"I've got a favor or two I can call in. It pays to have a little credit in the personnel bank,"

"Now, about that *wicked* issue," C. B. said as she turned to Tru, her eyes lidded in intent.

"Yes. There's a time and place, though. If the time is now, we might want to wait until we get back to your place or mine and after we've transported this stuff to the lab," Tru said, leaning toward C. B.'s waiting lips.

As their lips slightly touched, Tru's pager jangled emphatically on her hip. She grabbed at the screeching annoyance and looked at the number display.

"Don't go away," Tru said, getting to her feet. "I've got to call the station. Someone put a priority return on the call. I'll be right back," she said as she made her way out of the room and down to her car.

C. B. shrugged her shoulders and returned to the job of collecting the fire-starter samples. She finished filling her backpack and was ready to leave by the time Tru returned.

"What was it?" C. B. said as she walked to the hallway door where Tru stood.

"You wouldn't believe it in a million years."

"Try me," C. B. said, studying Tru's face.

"Mawson's in custody," Tru breathed and shook her head in disbelief.

"What? Mawson's dead. We were watching your

pathologist Houghin cut him in tiny pieces earlier today," C. B. insisted.

"That's what I thought too. But he's alive and in some little jail in the Ozarks. Got picked up in a speeding trap. The son of a bitch is alive. They checked his prints. The sheriff's office down there is transporting him up here in the morning," Tru said, letting her eyes go wide in amazement as she looked up into C. B.'s face.

"Then who in the hell were we looking at in the morgue?"

"I haven't a clue. I can tell you one thing. I'd better know who by the time I finish interrogating Mawson. Otherwise he's going to be one sorry, uncrispy SOB," Tru said in indignation. "Shit, shit, shit. I had an identified body. Now I may have an arsonist and the body is unidentified. I don't know if I'm getting ahead of the game or falling behind."

"Come on. Let's get this stuff to the lab and get a drink. Shall we?" C. B. offered.

"At least one," Tru said as they left the building. "Maybe two," she grumbled as they headed back downtown.

Chapter 14

Late Saturday morning Tru rolled over and snuggled her way closer to C. B. until she was curled spoon fashion against the other woman's back. The warm-skin-to-warm-skin touch caused C. B. to mumble lightly in her sleep. Tru raised her head and propped it up with her hand to watch C. B.'s face as she slept. A salt-and-pepper lock of hair had fallen over C. B.'s face and further softened the response of slumber. *It is a good face,* Tru thought. *So different from Marki's face. And she seems so different from*

Marki in so many ways. She smiled to herself as she began to understand how much she enjoyed the company, lovemaking, and sense of C. B. *I enjoy Marki too,* her mind insisted. *This could get very complicated.*

As if sensing watchful eyes on her, C. B. rolled over and looked up at Tru. "Good morning. And what are you up to?" C. B. said sleepily.

"I'm trying to make a decision."

"About what?" C. B. said, rousing herself to fuller attention.

"About whether or not we have time to make love again, shower, and have breakfast or brunch before we get to work," Tru said, shoving her actual musings to the back of her mind. She would keep them until time was available for thorough reflection.

C. B. turned away and took a quick peek at the clock radio on the nightstand. "It's after eleven. Seems as though those drinks and extracurricular activities have taken a toll on the morning. And as much as I regret having to say this" — she pulled Tru into her arms — "we don't have time to do all of that if we are to get everything done that you said we should try to do today."

"Is that the sound of rejection?"

"Not rejection. Think of it as delay, postponement, and a promise I'll keep anytime you say."

"With interest?"

"You want me to hold you to that?" Tru raised an eyebrow in the interest of seeking clarification.

"I should hope that you would," C. B. said. She pulled Tru closer. "Who needs brunch?"

* * * * *

157

"I'm going to call Dr. Houghin and see if she has anything for me. She might not be happy with a call on Saturday, but she'll forgive me," Tru said as she and C. B. walked to her car. *I've got to get a change of clothes too or start leaving some here. What am I thinking? I've never left a change of clothes with Marki.*

"Sounds right."

"After that, I'm going back to my apartment. I've got to feed my poor cat, Poupon. If I don't, he'll never forgive me and I'll be in danger of him leaving little attitude reminders on my bed. I'll check the computer disks I took from Mawson's apartment when we thought he was dead. I want to see if there is anything on them before I interrogate him." Tru opened the car door and sat down. The case felt like it was getting away from her.

The surprise reappearance of a live Mawson had spun the case in a new direction. It wasn't a matter of a fire-starter who unwittingly committed murder. Tru thought that the possibility of malicious and murderous hidden intent in the fires had grown to a certainty.

"Sounds like a full day," C. B. said, leaning into Tru's car window. It was Saturday and usually would have been a day off, but she'd decided not to dress for work. She figured anyone who saw her today in her blue jeans, work boots, chambray shirt, and pea jacket would still have to respond to her as an arson investigator once they saw her badge and identification card.

"No fuller than your day," Tru said as she touched C. B.'s hand.

"That's about the size of it. I want to find that call girl and talk to her. Then there's the matter of the laboratory's examination of the substances we found. I think I'm also going to try to backtrack and again talk to the owners of the buildings that burned. They should have completed the investigation questionnaires by now. Maybe they can shed some light on why our arsonist was targeting them, or maybe I can see if I missed anything else there. If you get anything from Mawson that sounds interesting" — C. B. lightly kissed Tru on the cheek — "page me. All right?"

"Consider it done. Do you want to meet back here this evening?" Tru asked as she put the car in gear.

"I was hoping you'd want to. As long as you're comfortable with the idea. I don't want you to feel pressured into spending all your time with me. I have to admit, I'm a bit concerned that you'll have regrets sneak up on you when Marki returns and disappear on me."

"I don't operate that way. Really. And Marki and I do have to have a long talk or two. That isn't going to take me from you."

"As long as you're sure," C. B. said, nodding to Tru as her car pulled away.

C. B. walked to her truck, wondering what the gist of the conversation might be between Marki and Tru. She knew that she was caught up in the middle of a firestorm and that Tru was at the burning center of it. It made her feel like she was twenty again, but she hoped she wasn't acting as dull witted as she had then. She certainly felt more impetuous, aroused, and immersed in desire than she had in years. She shook her head and decided not to worry about what she couldn't control as she drove to the fire marshal's arson unit chemical analysis laboratory.

Jerry Johnson looked up from the stainless-steel workbench as C. B. opened the plateglass door of the laboratory. He smiled at her, took off his glasses, and scooted his bench-high wheeled chair away from the table.

"Putting in a little overtime, C. B.?" he asked cheerily.

"No more than I have to," she said as she crossed the floor to where he sat. "No more than you do." C. B. watched him cross his long, thin legs and grinned at him as she noticed how much he looked like a lab-coated praying mantis as he hunched over his stool.

"Bullshit," Jerry insisted. "I've been keeping track. You put in more hours a week than any two of the other investigators with the fire marshal. I'm beginning to think you don't have a life of your own."

"Busy hands are happy hands," C. B. admonished.

"Maybe, but a happy home life is healthier."

"I do fine, Jerry. In fact, I'm great."

"I thought I detected a spring in your otherwise purposeful saunter. Found someone to melt that cold heart of yours, have we?" he prodded.

"Feeling rebuffed, Jerry?" C. B. quipped.

"Yeah. By you all the time, and by my wife only a little more frequently," Jerry responded in kind.

"Well, unless you intend to tell me your life story as it has unfolded since last week . . . Have you found anything in that mess of containers that will do me any good?"

"Now that you ask, I think I have," Jerry said, becoming all business. "Over here," he said, rolling his chair back to the stainless-steel table. "See these spectrographic printouts?"

"Yeah?"

"The first one indicates potassium nitrate. Fertilizer, to you. The second one is sulfuric acid, common vehicle battery acid. The third one shows traces of gasoline. I also picked up a trace of sugar in that tiny lump of charred cork you brought in," Jerry said, setting the slips of printout in front of C. B.

"Fertilizer, sugar, and battery acid? Not the normal sort of elements one finds in or around an electrical panel," C. B. mused.

"It might be if you wanted to blow it up," Jerry asserted.

"All right, Jerry. What am I dealing with here?"

"One smart cookie. A bit risky too. This arsonist is a pro. You weren't meant to find this stuff. He wasn't a bit sloppy when he made this little incendiary time bomb."

"Time bomb?"

"Yes, a time bomb. From the materials you recovered, I can reconstruct a possible scenario," Jerry assured C. B.

"What sort of scenario. What kind of bomb?"

"Sweet, neat, and simple. The guy was good. This whole setup relied on a chemical reaction. No

161

explosives of any kind. No genius work either. Real nice simple tools. How'd you know to look for this anyway?"

"I got lucky. There was a second fire," C. B. said, looking about the room. Her eyes came to rest on a box she'd carried in last night to the laboratory. "There's a chance the stuff in that box," she said, pointing, "contains the same residues. I had Linda and her dog come down from St. Joe. The dog sniffed the stuff out for me. But I might not have thought of that if an eyewitness to the second fire had been any less articulate about the explosion and flames. I got lucky."

"I'll say. You needed all the luck you could handle. Otherwise you might have passed both of them off as having been caused by faulty electrical panels."

"That's exactly what they looked like. I even had the utility provider electrician examine the panels. We'd both come to the conclusion that the fires were accidents. This information cinches the first arson as a murder," C. B. asserted. Mawson wouldn't be a partner at play anymore with the victim at the Genesse building. If he set the fire, he'd be charged with murder. She wanted to get to a phone and let Tru know what Jerry had discovered.

"I don't know. There are a lot easier ways to kill someone. A lot easier than waiting for this little gem to take charge."

"I was at a convention a few years back. It seems to me that I heard some New York fire marshal talking about this type of thing. Their arsonist had managed to burn down ten warehouses on the wharf before they could stop him. After his arrest, the guy was thrilled with all the media attention he received. He actually bragged to the investigators how he started the fires." C. B. shrugged in perplexity.

"He was proud of his work?"

"I guess so. Takes all kinds, doesn't it? Seems as though he used the cardboard tubes from paper towels, reinforced them with duct tape, and poured in potassium chlorate and some other combustible separated by a cork. Another vial contained an acid that would eat the cork. When the cork was sufficiently dissolved, the two unstable substances would mix, igniting a very hot, powerful fire. He hung some gas-filled balloons around the incendiary device, and when the fire touched them they fell to the floor and cooked the area. It also destroyed much of the evidence."

"Sounds like something our arsonist tried."

"Exactly. But our guy seems to have been a lot cagier. He placed the incendiary device next to an open electrical panel. The explosions and fires made it look like the fault was the panel — the lids blown off, extensive damage to the interior, and deep charring in the area all pointed to accident."

"Not anymore," Jerry assured her.

"Jerry, I need you to run tests on that second box of stuff. If you detect the same types of chemicals in it, we've got a bigger issue than a murdering arsonist. We've got a serial arsonist. Lots of people, particularly firefighters, could get hurt or killed if we don't put a stop to this," C. B. said anxiously. She didn't want anyone to go through what she'd experienced if she could help it.

"You sound like you're leaving," Jerry said, looking up at her.

"I am. I've got a witness to the second fire I need to talk to and a few other people. If I'm lucky, by the time you finish with your stuff I may have an idea who our arsonist is."

"Where will you be?"

"Here," C. B. said, tossing him her card. "Page me when you know for certain. The minute you know. I'll get hold of you," she said as she strode out of the room.

Jerry watched C. B. leave and turned back to his work with a heavy sigh. He envied C. B.'s active investigation style and the idea of actually hunting down the arsonist and arresting him. Nah, he thought as he walked to the second set of boxed evidence. It might not be as much fun as it sounded, and it could be dangerous. He gladly turned his attention back to his laboratory tools.

In her truck, C. B. called Tru's apartment. She let the phone ring until Tru's answering machine came on. C. B. left a quick message telling Tru she was going to try to find the call girl who saw the man running from the second fire. She also left Jerry Johnson's phone number for Tru to call and get the details from the analyst's own mouth.

Last night when she and Tru had talked about the witness, Tru had stated that sometimes witnesses know more than they ever say. Tru mentioned that it was important not to just let them talk, but with witnesses like a call girl it was necessary to try to break down the barricades of the distrust of authority.

C. B. hoped she could be persuasive as she headed her truck toward Overland Park and the drop-off address she'd secured from the cab company. She wondered what sort of house or apartment complex a call girl might pick. As she drove, she imagined that a sort of overstated, gauche opulence would fit the stereotype.

The house at 3100 Fifty-second Street in Overland Park was a modest ranch. C. B. noticed that it had what Realtors called curb appeal. The smartly placed, carved sandstones bracketed the walk up to the door and were overgrown with tiny green shrubbery. The front of the house was set off under the windows by sculptured cedar shrubs, which gave a slightly oriental flare as they marched back toward the fenced-in backyard. Tendrils of winding rosebushes guarded the front door. It was not what she had expected. She had not known what to expect a call girl to call home, but this certainly wasn't it.

As she climbed out of the truck, C. B. wondered if the manager at the cab company had made a mistake. There was only one way to find out. Maybe the mistake, she reasoned, was the catty little mouth of the hostess at the Golden Bull. C. B. figured that it wouldn't be the first time that rumor or innuendo was used by the small-minded and mean-spirited that made up far too much of the world.

She stood on the steps to the porch and hesitated before reaching out to ring the doorbell. She rehearsed her opening line once again inside her head, touched the bell, and waited. She rang it again when thirty seconds had passed. *Crap, maybe I should have called first to find out if she is at home,* C. B. thought ruefully.

Then the door opened wide so quickly that it

almost startled C. B. It wasn't the quickness of the opening of the door that truly startled her. It was the waiflike woman standing in front of her.

Jennie Dietz looked up at C. B. and struggled with her robe and the threat of the gushing wind at the doorway blowing it open to expose her nudeness. Her wide fawn eyes softened as they responded to C. B.'s compelling face.

"Yes?"

"Are you Jennifer Dietz?"

"Yes, I am. How may I help you?"

"I have some questions for you," C. B. said, remembering to reach into her hip pocket and pull out her identification badge. "I'm an arson investigator, and I believe you were witness to a fire the other evening."

"How did you find me? What do you want?" Jennie's eyes widened in alarm at the sight of the badge.

"I'm an arson investigator with the fire department, Ms. Dietz. I'm not a police officer. I only investigate fires." C. B. tried to calm Jennie Dietz's fears.

"Fire department?"

"Yes, Miss, if we could step inside for a minute," C. B. said, pulling her jacket collar up around her neck to protect it against the cold gusts of wind.

"Oh," Jennie said as she tried to clam herself. "Do come in." She moved back from the entrance and beckoned C. B. inside. "Sit down; I'll change and be back in a moment."

C. B entered the cozy living room where a small fire provided little real heat and a lot more atmosphere to the decor. She waited and wondered what Jennie might change into and whether she had violated investigative protocol by letting Jennie out of her sight. She didn't have to wonder long. Jennie quickly returned, wearing a loose-fitting white silk blouse and form-hugging faded jeans.

"Please, sit down," Jennie encouraged C. B. as she moved to sit in an overstuffed chair near the fire. Her complexion was flawless and translucent. A hint of pink lipstick heightened the color of her skin. She pulled her legs up into the chair, crossed them at the ankles which made her look even more youthful and diminutive. "Now, exactly how did you find me, and what is it you want?"

C. B. lowered herself into a Queen Anne chair across from Jennie. She looked at the small, vivacious woman and had the sensation that her six-foot frame was suddenly too large and clumsy.

"An employee at the restaurant thought they had recognized you when you came back in and called 911 about the fire. It was a small matter of calling the cab company to find out the drop-off point for the fare the driver picked up. I took a chance that you were the same person who called 911. I'm right, aren't I?"

"You are. But I don't see how I can be of further help. It's not against the law to leave once you've done everything you can, is it?" Jennie protested.

"No, it's not. What I'm interested in is if you can tell me more about the man you told the 911 operator you saw running from the building." C. B. took out a small notepad and leaned forward waiting for a response.

"It was dark. I might not have thought a thing about it, except he came running up the outside basement stairs after what sounded like an explosion." Jennie shifted in the chair and seemed to clasp her hands more firmly across her ankles.

"There were streetlights and some lights from the window fronts. Did you get a look at his face? I understand you eat rather often at the Golden Bull. Had you ever seen him before?"

"He was running, Miss . . ." Jennie faltered.

"Belpre, but you can call me C. B., if you wish."

"C. B.? Is that your name or part of some fire department investigative title?" Jennie reached up and smoothed a stray golden curl back into place.

"It's my name," C. B. said, chuckling.

"What does it stand for?"

"Nothing. Just C. B."

"Not Carol Beth, Clara Belle, Country Bound, or anything remotely related to a real word?" Jennie sat upright in the chair and crossed her legs. Her eyes danced in mirth as she watched perplexity play across C. B.'s face.

"Not one real word, simply and uncomplicatedly C. B."

"I seriously doubt that you're an uncomplicated woman, C. B."

"Extraordinarily uncomplicated. However, I feel as though you're trying to complicate my investigation by being evasive," C. B. responded in her best professional voice. She worked to ignore Jennie's flirting signals. *Some women*, C. B. reflected to herself.

"It was dark, and he moved so fast. I was alarmed at the sound, and then there was the fire. I'm afraid I didn't see anything other than that he was wearing a trench coat of some kind. It was dark in color," Jennie said shrugging hopelessly at C. B.

"Well, thanks for talking to me." C. B. rose from her chair and extended a hand to Jennie.

Jennie reached out and took the offered business card in her left hand and clasped C.B's outstretched hand with hers. "Thank you for stopping by. And if you ever have a chance, stop by again. I'd love to have you come over and tell me all about your work."

C. B.'s eyebrows almost followed her brain's full alert. She gently pulled her hand out of the tiny grip. "Call me if you think of anything. I can see myself to the door." She turned and walked purposefully down the hall and to the front door.

"Anytime."

C. B. turned around to see Jennie leaning against the wall of the hallway. She looked petite, pretty, and potentially dangerous.

C. B. coughed to clear her throat. "Thank you," she said. She opened and shut the door behind her.

The man in the black Buick LeSabre watched C. B. walk to her truck, unlock the door, and get in. He waited, his patience stretching to the breaking point as she jotted notes on a pad she held up in front of her. He pulled his car in behind her when she started the truck and drove it down the street. He kept a safe distance behind, using the other traffic as cover, and followed her to a fire department ladder-truck company downtown.

He looked at his watch and decided it would take him a little over forty minutes to get back to Jennie's house. It would be five o'clock, and the day would be heading toward darkness.

Chapter 15

"Dr. Houghin."

"Camellia, it's Tru North. Can you meet me at the lab or arrange to have one of your assistants meet with me at your office?" Tru asked as she sped around the slower moving traffic on Twelfth Street.

"What's up?"

"The craziest thing has happened. The guy we thought was Mawson, the very dead guy? Turns out he's not. Mawson was arrested yesterday driving his car down in the Ozarks. They're bringing him up here later this morning. That means I've got a lot of ground to cover before he gets here. I know it's asking a lot, but I need the report on the body that you examined yesterday. What are my chances?"

"Any other Saturday, your chances would be slim to none. However, under the circumstances, I think something can be arranged. I think Harry Waters is on call this weekend. I'll call him and make sure he meets you there. I'll be along as soon as I can," Camellia said as she hung up the phone.

"Thanks," Tru said into the dead air of the mobile phone. She turned south on Troost Avenue and headed toward Hospital Hill Park. She sped along under the I-70 underpass en route to the unassuming squat brick building that housed the coroner's office and the newly unidentified body.

She arrived fifteen minutes ahead of Harry Waters and spent an unpleasant time loitering in the coroner's office outer waiting area. Her impatience made her fidget and pace the length of the hallway until she heard the sounds of footsteps approaching from a distance. An anterior hallway door flew open, and an exasperated Dr. Harry Waters marched through in heavy work boots, plaid shirt, and overalls. He didn't look happy.

"What's this about our crispy being unidentified? Weren't you the one that found his wallet with the body?" Harry said as he passed by Tru and through the double-hinged doors of the complex.

"Goes to show you what happens when we expect the obvious. Stuff happens," Tru complained as she followed his bouncing stride down the hall.

"This couldn't have waited till Monday?" Harry shot at her over his shoulder.

"No, it couldn't. The real Mawson is on his way

to my jail as we speak. I want to know anything and everything about how, when, and why whoever you've got in cold storage might have died. I can't do a proper interview without knowing more than that some unlucky stiff melted into his rubber suit. If I wait for Monday, his attorney will have him out on bail and as far away from me as he can keep him."

"Whatever," Harry said as he unlocked his office door. "Let's see what we have for you." Harry switched on the fluorescent overheads, walked to his desk, and began sifting through a stack of reports in brown folders. "Here it is," he said, tossing Tru the report. "That's your copy. Keep it."

"Is Camellia coming?" Tru asked as she thumbed the pages.

"No. I told her I'd take care of you. However, I'd like to get back to working on my lawn as quickly as possible. I'd hoped to finish reseeding some bald areas this weekend. Some of us have a life you know," he said as he hovered near his desk.

"You want to nutshell this for me then? I can sit here and read it word for word and ask you questions as I go. Or you can fill me in on the high points, strange points, or anything you think might be helpful. Which do you think might get you back to your lawn quicker?" Tru said, letting her lips part in a feral smile.

"Shit," Harry said as he grabbed the official copy of the autopsy report from his desk and sat down in his chair. He opened the report and bent over the thirty pages of detail in front of him.

As she waited, Tru read over the highlighted notes Dr. Houghin had marked on her copy.

"OK, Mawson, rather, John Doe skeletal structure

and teeth indicate a male in his mid to late twenties; in life he might have weighed somewhere between 165 and 175 pounds, a medium build to thinnish man topping out at close to six feet tall. No sign of a history of broken bones, fractures, or childhood injuries. Pretty healthy except he appeared to have had both of his upper back molars recently removed. Probably cosmetic reasons. He had a hell of a lot of teeth in that mouth," Harry said, shifting in his chair.

"What?"

"He had a big mouth. Maybe that's why he died. Get it?"

Tru looked up at Harry without responding.

Harry Waters blanched at Tru's uncompromising, deadpan stare and looked back down at the report. "Anyway, lots of teeth, too many, or too large. Not uncommon in human beings really. It is a little unusual that his parents didn't take care of it when he was younger."

"Maybe they didn't have the money. It happens," Tru heard herself responding defensively. She shook it off. "Anything else? Anything having to do with the cause of death for example?

"My examination indicated that he was alive during the fire. There were signs of soot and smoke particles in and around the mouth and nose. He did not, as it first appeared, die from strangulation. Neither did he die from smoke inhalation. There was trauma to the cranium. Two blows, I figure. The skull showed intersecting fissures. Lastly, hematoma, some minor brain swelling, occurred. But it's my guess he died a few minutes after receiving the blow. There must have been heavy smoke in the room by the time he came to and found himself strung up in a death trap. Whoever killed him may have rendered him unconscious with the first blow and, intending to or not, finished him with the second one. You find any weapons at the crime scene?" Harry said looking up at Tru.

"If I had known this — the guy's height, approximate age, and weight — I would have known sooner that it wasn't Mawson."

"Would that have been helpful?"

"I don't know now. Anyway, thanks Harry. You can go back to your lawn. You've given me a lot to think about. Particularly where patience as a virtue is concerned," Tru said as she rose to leave.

"Pardon?"

"Nothing. Just something I need to work on," Tru said as she left Harry sitting at this desk.

On the drive to her apartment, Tru mulled over her recurrent tendency to be impatient. She chastised herself for rushing out of the autopsy with C. B. She realized that her libido had overridden her good sense and investigative skills. Her conscience nagged at her all the way to the parking lot behind her apartment.

Tru sat at her computer in her apartment and loaded the A drive with one of the four floppies she'd secured from the Mawson apartment. She engaged the virus protection lock on her computer and hit ENTER. Mawson had used slightly more sophisticated software than what Tru owned, but the disk was still compatible. The program was password protected. Tru took a gamble and cross-loaded the disk into a read file in her hard drive. Once loaded, she backdoored the program and reset the password as *Mawson*. It worked.

"Lucky guess," she breathed. She had been hoping that Mawson wasn't a techno-paranoid. He'd been just cautious enough to lock curious eyes out of his files but wasn't paranoid about someone getting hold of his disks. She quickly scanned each file, trying to find a key word or two that might indicate his scheming and strategies. The program contained ledger sheets, financial accounts information, copies of memoranda, and a personal journal.

The journal revealed that Mawson had worked as an assistant city finance officer for six years and that he had hated his job. He referred to working with local banks, federal loans and grants, and the soliciting business investors in the city as shit work. His journal contained page after page of ranting against the questionable practices the city sometimes engaged in when backing renovation and development schemes of its friends.

His rantings were interspersed with his concern for the disadvantages faced by pint-size investors, storefront entrepreneurs, and midsize project developers. They would come to his office with hat in hand, he'd give them the party line, and he'd see disappointment reflected in their faces. He'd sympathized with them. Complained to himself and his journal that the big guys always got the big breaks and the little guys got left out, just like him. He'd been watching for years as the power brokers made money and he earned salary. He was angry. Angry enough that he had contemplated quitting and seeking an investment partnership with some money and a lot of energy. But he hadn't quit.

The journal entries and financial accounts showed that he'd figured out how to have his cake and eat it too. He worked for the city, got inside information, and shared it with a silent partner or group he referred to as R. R.

"Railroad?" Tru asked the journal entry. "He's invested in the railroad?"

R. R. was a man or corporation that was as desperate and angry as Mawson and as hungry. They worked together as a team. Mawson had the information, and R. R. had the funds. Together they took advantage of every whisper, suggestion, and piece of investment-source information that came Mawson's way as a trusted city employee. No bid was let for renovation or construction in the West Bottoms and River Quay without their knowledge.

"Bet his bank account looks healthy now," Tru mused. The hours passed swiftly as she stared into the screen. She read the files carefully; she saw his resentment with his failures and benign neglect of his supervisors. He'd become a man with a mission. Intent on getting over his compartmentalized bureaucratic existence, he'd plotted and planned his financial revenge.

Staring into the computer screen, she didn't hear his approach on padded feet. Something brushed up against her leg. Startled out of her reverie, she looked down in time to see Poupon meow plaintively up to her.

"Poor baby. I meant to feed you the minute I got home. Come on, let's see what sort of cat delectables we have in the cupboard." Tru picked Poupon up and walked out to the small efficiency kitchen in her apartment. As she sauntered past the phone she noticed that the message light was flashing wildly, indicating a fistful of messages waiting for her. She squinted at the recorder in guilt.

"First, I feed Poupon," Tru told the angry little blinking light. "Then you can tell me the trouble I'm in and with whom."

As Poupon purred contentedly over his meal, Tru sat next to the phone and listened to the messages on the machine. There were eight callers. Garvan wanted to know where she'd run off to, Jones had called twice wanting updates on the investigation, and two different phone companies wanted her to switch to their services. Marki had called three times, in each call her voice sounding more and more a strange mix of irritation and questioning.

Tru winced when she heard Marki's voice in the last message as she indicated that she would be flying home Wednesday and intended to sit down with Tru and have a long conversation. Marki specified that there were things they needed to straighten out and go forward with to move their relationship to a solid stage.

Tru grabbed her briefcase and headed for the door. She didn't want to think about the complications of Marki's phone calls and was glad that she'd avoided them. As her hand turned the doorknob, the phone began to ring. It made her jump. Feeling foolish and a bit cowardly, she fairly ran out of the apartment.

* * * * *

Tru and Tom Garvan sat in the interview room at the jail and waited for a county corrections officer to bring Darrell Mawson to her. The room's door opened and a husky, orange-suited man in handcuffs and belly chain was led in by a brown-suited officer.

"Sit down, Mr. Mawson," Tru directed the puzzled man.

"I don't think so," Mawson responded. His reddening face made his red hair and freckles violently clash with the standard orange jail attire. Orange wasn't his color. "I want to know how in the hell you can have me arrested for stealing my own car? My attorney will skin you alive," he bellowed and surged toward her. The corrections officer vigorously jerked on the belly chain to restrain his charge.

"Mr. Mawson," Tru said in a level, commanding tone. "If you don't sit down and talk to me in a civil fashion, the next time you see me will be at your murder trial." Tru shifted in the chair and waited for the idea to soak into Mawson's awareness.

"Murder trial? Don't tell me you're going to charge me with my own murder now too?" Mawson laughed menacingly.

"Don't be absurd, Mawson. You're here because a man is dead. He had your ID with him, and your car was missing. For the last two days I've thought you were the poor trussed-up and toasted bastard. You set the fire in the Genesse Exchange to eliminate a co-conspirator in your securities and investment frauds. You got too greedy for your own good, but you weren't very lucky. You didn't get far enough away and you got caught because I had an APB out on your car. The only thing you've got left to decide, as far as I'm concerned, is how to work with your lawyer to see if he can save you from the death penalty by lethal injection. I'd suggest a plea of temporary insanity."

Shock and comprehension spread across Mawson's face. His body seemed to crumble as he walked unsteadily toward the metal chair opposite Tru and Garvan. All the indignation had drained out of him. The corrections officer steadied him to keep him from toppling over and guided him down into the chair. He wobbled heavily into the chair and stared at the tabletop.

"I don't understand."

"What part don't you understand?" Tru asked, dropping her voice to a whisper. She shoved a waiver-of-rights form toward him and waited for him to refocus.

"Everything was fine. I was on vacation, fishing. I hadn't been fishing in years," Mawson said, looking up at Tru. "I wouldn't kill anybody. It had to be suicide. But why frame me for murder? If he wanted to die, fine. But why frame me for murder? I never did anything but help him make money."

"Sign the waiver, Mawson," Tru redirected and turned on the tape recorder in her briefcase. Her face a blank of emotions, she turned to Garvan and raised an eyebrow.

"Sure, why not," Mawson said, reaching for the paper and the pen Tru offered. "I tell you, I didn't kill him. The crazy bastard was insane. And I'll tell you this, I may have violated securities exchange laws, but I'm not going down for murder," Mawson asserted as he signed the waiver.

"Who was he, Mawson? Who was your so-called crazy partner who cooked himself in the Genesse?"

"Stupid fuck. He made bad investments. It was like he started to unravel after he'd sunk too much money into some stupid West Bottoms speculation. I should have seen it coming. He got worse when the city started to conduct an unscheduled securities investigation. That started last month. Shit, detective, I took a vacation to get away from him coming to my apartment and all the lunatic phone calls. He couldn't, wouldn't just let the thing run its own course. Fucking securities investigator was fresh out of law school. He couldn't have found his ass in the dark if he'd used both hands. He wouldn't have found a thing. I know, I covered our tracks using every trick in the book." Mawson's tirade subsided, his body slouched forward, and he placed his head on the table.

"Mawson. I need a name. We have to identify the body."

Darrell Mawson raised his lethargic head and focused red-rimmed eyes on Tru. "Rinhart. Fucking crazy Mister Super Endowment, Ronald Rinhart. He lived off the silk purse his father left him. But he'd started to go through it pretty fast in the last few years. He, we, were beginning to see some real money with my skills, his money, and a bit of inside information. Then he goes and does this, this setting me up for securities fraud when he commits suicide. That takes the cake, doesn't it, detective?" Mawson stared fixedly at his hands.

"It certainly does," Tru said as her mind went spinning down corridors of possibilities. She looked at

Tom for confirmation of her memory that Ronald Rinhart was the owner of the Genesse Exchange, the building where the body was found.

"Right," Tom said in a hushed whisper as he nodded his head.

"Just for the sake of argument, who was the securities investigator he was worried about?" Tru said as she turned back to Mawson.

"Kenneth Lester. Came out of Columbia University. Shit, he'll probably get a promotion out of this," Mason said, lowering his head to the table again.

"Do you know if he had any recent dental work?"

Mawson's head snapped up and glared at Tru. "That's a strange question, detective."

"Humor me. Do you know if he'd been to a dentist recently?"

"Now that you ask, seems to me the last time I talked to him he was complaining about his nose feeling numb from Novocain. I shrugged it off, figured that he was trying to make an excuse for his usual bumbling. Why do you ask?"

"Then I don't think he's going to get that promotion," Tru said as she handed Garvan the list of questions they'd previously planned to ask Mawson and the case file. "Mr. Mawson, we're going to leave you for right now. I'll be in touch. But right now I've got a few loose ends to tie up," she said as she rose from the table and motioned for Garvan to follow. She wanted to get to Rinhart before he caught wind of Mawson's confinement at city jail.

"You're not really going to charge me with murder are you?" Mawson asked as he watched Tru walk to the secured jail door.

"That remains to be seen, Mawson. The more you help the detective here with what he wants to know, the more we can tell the district attorney about your willingness to cooperate," Tru said as she and Garvan walked toward the steel security doors. "By the way, do you know what bad investments he made in the Bottoms?"

"Yeah. You'll love it," Mawson chuckled as the electronically controlled door sprang to life in front of the detectives. "The stupid bastard bought one of those hell houses. Cost him a bundle because he even spent money to renovate. Thought he'd make his money back in one Halloween. Can you imagine?"

"I'm beginning to," Tru breathed.

"Too bad the son of a bitch is dead. I sure as hell could kill him now," Mawson yelled as Tru and Garvan stepped through the sliding bars. The heavy jarring clang of the electronic doors closing resonated on the concrete floor as Tru and Garvan hurried down the corridor.

Chapter 16

"Get some uniforms and get over to his residence. Have a couple of units go over to the Genesse building. He might have gone back there without permission."

"Where are you going to be?" Garvan asked.

"I'm going to go pick up C. B. She'll want to be in on this. The minute I get her, I'll head to the Genesse. Have the patrol units hang back. This will probably turn into a stakeout unless you catch him at home. It might be a long night, and I don't want him spooked. Let's get the cuffs on him tonight, shall we?" Tru directed as she and Garvan emerged from the building, jogged across the parking lot, and into the fading light of the day.

"You got it." Garvan waved as he trotted toward his unmarked car.

"Unit 81 to dispatch," Tru said as she grabbed the microphone from its concealment under the front seat. She sneaked a quick look at her watch and noticed that time was marching toward six in the evening.

"Go ahead," dispatch responded.

"Call the midtown fire marshal's office and find out if Investigator Belpre's available. If she's not at her office, I have a cellular phone number and resid —"

"No need," the dispatcher interrupted, "I've a message from Belpre for you. Call me on your cell."

Tru laid down the radio microphone and punched in the dispatch number. "What's the message?" she asked the responding dispatcher. She waited until she was forwarded to the dispatcher who had the message.

"Wants you to meet her at something called the Thirteenth Street Terrible Tombs in the Bottoms. Said she had some important information about a case."

"I bet I know what that's about. She doesn't know I've already beaten her to the punch," Tru chuckled to the dispatcher. "Thanks. If she calls back, tell her I'm on my way."

* * * * *

185

Dark had nestled into the lowlands of the Bottoms by the time Tru turned her car off the viaduct and onto the off ramp toward the stockyards. She made her way down Mulberry to the corner of Thirteenth Street and pulled the car over to the curb.

"Well, shit," she breathed as she looked down Thirteenth Street and the lines of cars stacked at the curbs and searching for parking spaces. "Damn Halloween and haunted houses," she cursed in exasperation.

Adult-size goblins, ghouls, space creatures, and plastic-faced movie heroes wandered in thick throngs along the street. Six days before Halloween, and Tru could see that the city revelers were in full costume and full swing. Their annual party and relatively safe grim festival had once again been redirected to the Bottoms. For more than ten years it had been a clean, orderly logic. No hell nights for Kansas City like those that made Detroit a death trap. The regularly predictable and scheduled havoc would be allowed to happen, but only in a controlled district. The hell houses were decorated, festooned, and filled with creeping horrors to satisfy the macabre humor of the crowds. Most of the streets surrounding the hell houses were blocked to keep the carousers and cars from meeting accidentally and creating real ghosts for the night.

Tru looked at the noisy, milling flocks of people in exasperation. She figured it would take her more time than she wanted to spare to reach C. B. and the Terrible Tombs. She was not happy and decided to let C. B. know about it the minute she caught up with her.

This is that duplication of effort I told her I didn't want us to get into. Tru exited the car and started to make her way through the ghoul-filled street.

Teenagers, smaller children, and adults ran, mingled, jostled, and swirled around her. Several stared at her as though she were out of place or a specter without the decency to guard her real face. Then it came to her, it might not be too hard to spot C. B. She wouldn't be wearing any costume either. The diversity of the bizarre would work for her, and if she could get to the Terrible Tombs house, she thought she ought to be able to spot C. B. at a distance.

Walking along, she looked up, saw her cue, and sprinted toward the building whose banner declared it the Terrible Tombs. Two double lines of customers crowded the doorways into the make-believe haunted house.

Tru searched the faces and the masks of those closest to her. She looked up and down the sidewalk without spotting C. B. Finally, Tru looked to the far side of the street and squinted into the darkness under the viaduct to see if C. B. had chosen to wait there instead of brave the crowds. But C. B. was nowhere to be found.

At a loss as to what to do next, Tru stood in front of the Terrible Tombs house of horrors and waited. The idea of wasting time trying to look for C. B. or wait for her to arrive from goddess-knew-where irritated her. People pushed rudely by her and elicited foul looks from her as they pressed by. She took a cigarette out of her jacket pocket, lit it, stood next to the building, and tried to keep out of the way of the foot traffic.

PA systems blared music, warbles of glee, ghostly howls, and sporadic gibberish over her head. It sounded for all the world as though the minions of hell were loose at the bottom of the river's bluff. Someone jostled her from behind. As she turned to confront the black-cloaked offender, he grabbed her right arm and thrust a solid blunt object into her back.

"Don't move," he said in a low, threatening tone. "I could kill you now and slip into panicked bystanders without ever being seen or heard from again. But you'd only die a little quicker than the other two."

"What other two?" Tru asked quietly as she tried to sneak a peek at the masked man behind her. His hand crushed down on her arm, making her wince.

"Don't get cute. I'll take you to them. Just remember to keep smiling. We wouldn't want these folks to think you're not having any fun," he said as he pulled her down the walkway to the side of the building.

The darkened alley swallowed the light and muffled the sounds from the street as the man shoved Tru in front of him. He heaved her forward and slammed her against the wall. The shove caused Tru to slam her right shoulder and side of her head into the brick construction near the fire escape. Dazed, she could feel him reach for the Glock .44 under her jacket and rip it from its holster.

"Don't want you to get any ideas," he snickered thinly.

"What makes you think I have any ideas, Rinhart?" Tru asked as she tried to stand up. She never saw the slap coming. It hit her like a hammer and reeled her back hard against the brick. The second blow dropped her down into the cobbled alley pavement.

"Shut up," he bellowed. "If you don't keep your mouth shut and get on your feet right now, I'll give you something that'll keep you down there for good," he threatened. "Stand up," he growled as he grabbed her arm and pulled her roughly to her feet. "Now get down there," he said as he pushed her toward a set of stairs leading down to the building's basement.

At the basement door he viciously grabbed the back of her neck and slammed her face into the side of the cold, concrete wall. She could hear him fishing around in his clothes looking for something. Then she heard the sound of a heavy tumbler as a key turned in the lock. He reasserted his grasp on her neck, pulled her back toward him, and pushed her through the door and into the empty blackness of the basement.

"A little farther. My guests have probably been getting a bit cold down here while we waited for you. Not to worry. It will start to warm up soon enough."

"Comedian," Tru dared the angry whisper.

"I said, keep your mouth shut." He landed two sharp blows on her back with the butt of his weapon. "Don't you ever learn?"

Tru faltered under the pummeling, tripped, and nearly fell to her knees. He fell forward on her and grabbed her by the throat. With his breath on her neck and his heavy body bearing down on her, his hands squeezed and choked her.

In the cover of the dark and the intensity of his suffocating hold, Tru reached for the knife near the empty holster. She slipped it out of its case as he stood up and jerked her to her feet.

"You aren't one of those bitches that has to have the last word, are you?" he asked as he pulled her toward him.

He didn't hear the hushed *snitch* sound of the blade flicking open in her hand. He didn't see her arm thrust forward or the way she marshaled all her strength to ram the blade into him. He did feel the cold thrust of the blade as she pushed it in deep.

"Word, Rinhart," she said as she used both hands to twist the blade up and deep into his chest.

She heard his gasp as he staggered under the shock of the blade sliding toward its fatal destination. They toppled backward as he recoiled against the lethal slice. He struck at her in pain and panic. Tru grabbed for his hand as he tried to hit her with the butt of the gun. She grappled with him for the gun and managed to take it from him before he could use it.

He used his size and remaining power to toss her away from him. The gun slipped from her fingers as she fell against the floor. She scrambled to her feet on the slick-mucked surface. She staggered, hobbled and dashed as fast as she could to get away from him.

She heard the soft thud of his body and a moan as he fell to the floor. Then the sound of two rapid shots split the air. She dove sightlessly down to the floor. The soft, whizzing buzz of a bullet passed her face as she landed on the unforgiving concrete. She rolled into a heap and lay as still as she could, listening. The noise from the street outside the basement stairwell was muffled. No shadow rose to cover the faint light beyond where Tru crouched. Listening intently, she heard the sounds of movement subside behind her.

She waited. Holding her breath, she strained her ears to detect where and when he might come for her. Long minutes passed, and nothing moved in the blackened space. She shifted and rose gingerly from where she'd hid. She listened some more.

"Rinhart," she called out to the darkness. Not a sound. Slowly, her heart beating in her throat, she walked back toward the place she had left him.

As she approached the opened doorway, she tripped over a shadow on the floor. It didn't move. She reached a shaking hand into her jacket pocket and flicked the cigarette lighter.

In the puny glow, Rinhart lay spread among the basement trash. The blood from the wound under his breastbone spread dark and wet across his body. She bent down and took her Glock from his waistband and his .38 from his hand.

Tru turned Rinhart over and searched through the large folds of the draping black costume he'd worn. In a deep inner pocket she found a small, high-powered flashlight. She turned it on and moved the light to the grotesque mask, reached out, and lifted it off the man's face to reveal Rinhart's slack features and closed eyes. She rolled him over on his face, took the handcuffs from her belt, and securely snapped them on his wrists. She wasn't taking any chances.

Tru staggered to her feet, held the light in front of her, and lurched down the hallway he'd meant for her to go. Twenty feet farther down the hallway Tru found a large wooden door bolted shut. She lifted the bolt from its rest. Her hands were bruised and bloody from their forced encounter with brick and cement.

Sudden movement at the far end of the room caused her to raise the light and Glock in quick aim at the sound. Then she saw them. In the startled glare of the small flashlight, Tru saw C. B. and another woman tied back-to-back sitting on the floor.

"C. B.," she called, running toward them. "What the hell?"

Tru jerked the gag from C. B.'s mouth as C. B. tried to talk in strained and strangled alarm.

"The box," C. B. said, her throat and mouth constricted in panic, "stop it."

"What?" Tru said, puzzled.

"There, up there." C. B. swallowed to relieve her sore throat. "The electrical panel, fire." She jerked her head upward.

Comprehension kicked in, and Tru turned the flashlight to the wall and the ceiling above the place where they huddled.

Ten balloons hung over them next to the electrical panel. The panel was open, and a cylindrical device nestled among the fuses and cable connections.

"Oh, shit!" Tru set the flashlight on the floor near C. B.'s hips and frantically grabbed at her knife to free the women from their ropes.

"I don't think there's time!" C. B. exclaimed.

"There has to be. I'm not dying this way, and neither are you," Tru declared as she frantically worked on the ropes holding C. B. She looked at the other woman. The young woman moaned in apprehension.

"Run," C. B. throatily commanded.

"Like hell," Tru said, leaning over as she gave C. B. a quick kiss and came to a decision.

Tru dropped the knife, stood up, and took three steps over to the electrical panel. *Ignorance is bliss,* she thought hopefully to herself and grabbed the device.

"No!" C. B. cried out, knowing the device could explode in Tru's hands and set her afire.

Tru ignored her and ran in the remembered direction of the door. The faint sound of the partyers whiffed toward her as she skidded through the opening. Expecting the impact to detonate the thing, she cocked her arm and heaved the device as far down the hall as she could. Nothing happened. She stood in the darkened doorway in surprise and shock. Nerves frayed to the breaking point, she peered down into the dark.

Suddenly a small eruption blasted through the hallway. The abrupt impact sent her hurtling back into the room.

"Tru!" She heard C. B.'s anxious voice.

"It's all right. I'm all right," Tru said as she stood up and looked at the quickly extinguishing flames at the far end of the brick-and-concrete hallway. "There no real fuel for it. It's a tiny tempest in the tombs," she said as she walked unsteadily toward the light that held C. B.

Chapter 17

"You look like hell," Garvan said as he watched the emergency medical technician examine Tru.

"Thanks. I can always count on you to help me see the brighter side." Tru winced as the EMT dabbed astringent on her scraped forehead. "How are the others?"

"Fine. The other ambulance crew is dealing with them. Seems it's mostly cold and cuts from the binding of the ropes. The EMT had a hell of a time getting that arson investigator to sit still long enough for him to take care of her. She seems more concerned about you than herself. Course, looking at you I can understand why."

"Who's the other woman?" Tru asked ignoring his comment.

"An eyewitness to the second fire. Seems she knew the guy. Said he had been like a mentor to her. Do call girls have mentors?" Garvan asked, his smile going askew.

"I don't believe I ever heard it called that. Ouch!" Tru exclaimed as the EMT tried to look at her scalp wounds. "Are you about done?" she complained.

"For now," the exasperated EMT advised. "You really should go to the hospital and get those injures looked at."

"Later. I promise. I'll go later." As the EMT jumped back inside the ambulance, Tru shifted on her jacket and stood up using Garvan's arm for balance.

"Steady. You're not ready to run any races yet," he scolded.

"OK," Tru said reluctantly. "You may have a point. So, did the coroner take Rinhart's body?"

"No body to take. He's alive," Garvan said. Surprise spread over Tru's face. "Must be one tough son of a bitch, too. I had the first ambulance haul him out of here after we got you and your friends topside. Last I heard, they thought he'd make it. No thanks to you and that little knife."

"Had it since I was a rookie. Good thing too. This might have gone real different."

"Go on home. We can finish up here without you. Take a long, warm bath, have a drink or two, put on some music, and relax," Garvan said, touching Tru lightly on her shoulder.

"Parenting me now, are you?"

"Just good sound advice."

"In a minute. I want to talk to C. B. Then I promise to take care of myself and leave you to the dirty work of cleaning up," Tru said as she walked toward the ambulance where C. B. and the call girl waited.

A young patrol officer approached the call girl as Tru walked to C. B.'s side. "Jennie Dietz," he said politely. "The detective over there would like to talk to you for a minute. If you could come with me, it won't take long."

Tru nodded to the officer and the young woman as they walked to where Garvan was standing. She turned around and smiled at C. B. and Tru as she followed the officer.

"Are you all right?" C. B. asked, solicitously taking Tru's hand.

"I've been better. But it's nothing that Garvan said a long warm bath, a cozy drink, and relaxation wouldn't cure. I wouldn't mind getting my mind off these aches and pains," Tru said, sensing her body's trounced muscles tightening in soreness. "Any idea where we might find something like that?"

"I've an idea or two. You look like you'll need time to recuperate before you try anything that's too strenuous again," C. B. said as she led Tru away from the bustle of activity.

"I'm not totally debilitated," Tru assured C. B.

They walked under the overpass and into the dark to where C. B. had driven her truck to meet Jennie and where Rinhart made her his second prisoner. C. B. opened the passenger door and helped Tru up into the seat.

"Well," C. B. said, touching Tru's face with her fingertips. "If you're not totally debilitated after the bath and drinks, we'll see if we can think of something to do so you get the feeling of relaxation you deserve."

"Deal," Tru said, flashing a mischievous conspiratorial grin at C. B.

A few of the publications of
THE NAIAD PRESS, INC.
P.O. Box 10543   Tallahassee, Florida 32302
Phone (850) 539-5965
Toll-Free Order Number: 1-800-533-1973
Web Site: WWW.NAIADPRESS.COM
Mail orders welcome. Please include 15% postage.
Write or call for our free catalog which also features an
incredible selection of lesbian videos.

BAD MOON RISING by Barbara Johnson. 208 pp. 2nd Colleen
Fitzgerald mystery.   ISBN 1-56280-211-9 $11.95

RIVER QUAY by Janet McClellan. 208 pp. 3rd Tru North
mystery.   ISBN 1-56280-212-7   11.95

ENDLESS LOVE by Lisa Shapiro. 272 pp. To believe, once
again, that love can be forever.   ISBN 1-56280-213-5   11.95

FALLEN FROM GRACE by Pat Welch. 256 pp. 6th Helen Black
mystery.   ISBN 1-56280-209-7   11.95

THE NAKED EYE by Catherine Ennis. 208 pp. Her lover in the
camera's eye . . .   ISBN 1-56280-210-0   11.95

OVER THE LINE by Tracey Richardson. 176 pp. 2nd Stevie
Houston mystery.   ISBN 1-56280-202-X   11.95

JULIA'S SONG by Ann O'Leary. 208 pp. Strangely
disturbing . . . strangely exciting.   ISBN 1-56280-197-X   11.95

LOVE IN THE BALANCE by Marianne K. Martin. 256 pp.
Weighing the costs of love . . .   ISBN 1-56280-199-6   11.95

PIECE OF MY HEART by Julia Watts. 208 pp. All the
stuff that dreams are made of —   ISBN 1-56280-206-2   11.95

MAKING UP FOR LOST TIME by Karin Kallmaker. 240 pp.
Nobody does it better . . .   ISBN 1-56280-196-1   11.95

GOLD FEVER by Lyn Denison. 224 pp. By author of *Dream*
Lover.   ISBN 1-56280-201-1   11.95

WHEN THE DEAD SPEAK by Therese Szymanski. 224 pp. 2nd
Brett Higgins mystery.   ISBN 1-56280-198-8   11.95

FOURTH DOWN by Kate Calloway. 240 pp. 4th Cassidy James
mystery.   ISBN 1-56280-205-4   11.95

A MOMENT'S INDISCRETION by Peggy J. Herring. 176 pp.
There's a fine line between love and lust . . .   ISBN 1-56280-194-5   11.95

CITY LIGHTS/COUNTRY CANDLES by Penny Hayes. 208 pp.
About the women she has known . . .   ISBN 1-56280-195-3   11.95

POSSESSIONS by Kaye Davis. 240 pp. 2nd Maris Middleton
mystery.   ISBN 1-56280-192-9   11.95

A QUESTION OF LOVE by Saxon Bennett. 208 pp. Every
woman is granted one great love.   ISBN 1-56280-205-4   11.95

RHYTHM TIDE by Frankie J. Jones. 160 pp.   . . . to desire
passionately and be passionately desired.   ISBN 1-56280-189-9   11.95

PENN VALLEY PHOENIX by Janet McClellan. 208 pp. 2nd
Tru North Mystery.   ISBN 1-56280-200-3   11.95

BY RESERVATION ONLY by Jackie Calhoun. 240 pp. A
chance for true happiness.   ISBN 1-56280-191-0   11.95

OLD BLACK MAGIC by Jaye Maiman. 272 pp. 9th Robin
Miller mystery.   ISBN 1-56280-175-9   11.95

LEGACY OF LOVE by Marianne K. Martin. 240 pp. Women
will do anything for her . . .   ISBN 1-56280-184-8   11.95

LETTING GO by Ann O'Leary. 160 pp. Laura, at 39, in love
with 23-year-old Kate.   ISBN 1-56280-183-X   11.95

LADY BE GOOD edited by Barbara Grier and Christine Cassidy.
288 pp. Erotic stories by Naiad Press authors.   ISBN 1-56280-180-5   14.95

CHAIN LETTER by Claire McNab. 288 pp. 9th Carol Ashton
mystery.   ISBN 1-56280-181-3   11.95

NIGHT VISION by Laura Adams. 256 pp. Erotic fantasy romance
by "famous" author.   ISBN 1-56280-182-1   11.95

SEA TO SHINING SEA by Lisa Shapiro. 256 pp. Unable to resist
the raging passion . . .   ISBN 1-56280-177-5   11.95

THIRD DEGREE by Kate Calloway. 224 pp. 3rd Cassidy James
mystery.   ISBN 1-56280-185-6   11.95

WHEN THE DANCING STOPS by Therese Szymanski. 272 pp.
1st Brett Higgins mystery.   ISBN 1-56280-186-4   11.95

PHASES OF THE MOON by Julia Watts. 192 pp. . . . . hungry
for everything life has to offer.   ISBN 1-56280-176-7   11.95

BABY IT'S COLD by Jaye Maiman. 256 pp. 5th Robin Miller
mystery.   ISBN 1-56280-156-2   10.95

CLASS REUNION by Linda Hill. 176 pp. The girl from her
past . . .   ISBN 1-56280-178-3   11.95

DREAM LOVER by Lyn Denison. 224 pp. A soft, sensuous,
romantic fantasy.   ISBN 1-56280-173-1   11.95

FORTY LOVE by Diana Simmonds. 288 pp. Joyous, heart-
warming romance.   ISBN 1-56280-171-6   11.95

IN THE MOOD by Robbi Sommers. 160 pp. The queen of
erotic tension!   ISBN 1-56280-172-4   11.95

SWIMMING CAT COVE by Lauren Douglas. 192 pp. 2nd
Allison O'Neil Mystery.   ISBN 1-56280-168-6   11.95

THE LOVING LESBIAN by Claire McNab and Sharon Gedan.
240 pp. Explore the experiences that make lesbian love unique.
                                           ISBN 1-56280-169-4   14.95

COURTED by Celia Cohen. 160 pp. Sparkling romantic
encounter.   ISBN 1-56280-166-X   11.95

SEASONS OF THE HEART by Jackie Calhoun. 240 pp. Romance
through the years.   ISBN 1-56280-167-8   11.95

K. C. BOMBER by Janet McClellan. 208 pp. 1st Tru North
mystery.   ISBN 1-56280-157-0   11.95

LAST RITES by Tracey Richardson. 192 pp. 1st Stevie Houston
mystery.   ISBN 1-56280-164-3   11.95

EMBRACE IN MOTION by Karin Kallmaker. 256 pp. A whirlwind
love affair.   ISBN 1-56280-165-1   11.95

HOT CHECK by Peggy J. Herring. 192 pp. Will workaholic Alice
fall for guitarist Ricky?   ISBN 1-56280-163-5   11.95

OLD TIES by Saxon Bennett. 176 pp. Can Cleo surrender to a
passionate new love?   ISBN 1-56280-159-7   11.95

LOVE ON THE LINE by Laura DeHart Young. 176 pp. Will Stef
win Kay's heart?   ISBN 1-56280-162-7   11.95

DEVIL'S LEG CROSSING by Kaye Davis. 192 pp. 1st Maris
Middleton mystery.   ISBN 1-56280-158-9   11.95

COSTA BRAVA by Marta Balletbo Coll. 144 pp. Read the book,
see the movie!   ISBN 1-56280-153-8   11.95

MEETING MAGDALENE & OTHER STORIES by
Marilyn Freeman. 144 pp. Read the book, see the movie!
                                           ISBN 1-56280-170-8   11.95

SECOND FIDDLE by Kate 208 pp. 2nd P.I. Cassidy James
mystery.   ISBN 1-56280-169-6   11.95

LAUREL by Isabel Miller. 128 pp. By the author of the beloved
Patience and Sarah.   ISBN 1-56280-146-5   10.95

LOVE OR MONEY by Jackie Calhoun. 240 pp. The romance of
real life.   ISBN 1-56280-147-3   10.95

These are just a few of the many Naiad Press titles — we are the oldest and
largest lesbian/feminist publishing company in the world. We also offer an
enormous selection of lesbian video products. Please request a complete
catalog. We offer personal service; we encourage and welcome direct mail
orders from individuals who have limited access to bookstores carrying our
publications.